The
Newspaper
Club

the Newspaper Club

BETH VRABEL

Illustrations by Paula Franco

RP|KIDS
PHILADELPHIA

Copyright © 2020 by Beth Vrabel
Interior and cover illustrations copyright © 2020 by Paula Franco
Cover copyright © 2020 by Hachette Book Group, Inc.

Running Press Kids
Hachette Book Group
1290 Avenue of the Americas, New York, NY 10104
www.runningpress.com/rpkids
@RP_Kids

Printed in the United States

First Edition: March 2020

Published by Running Press Kids, an imprint of Perseus Books, LLC, a subsidiary of Hachette Book Group, Inc. The Running Press Kids name and logo is a trademark of the Hachette Book Group.

The Hachette Speakers Bureau provides a wide range of authors for speaking events. To find out more, go to www.hachettespeakersbureau.com or call (866) 376-6591.

The publisher is not responsible for websites (or their content) that are not owned by the publisher.

Print book cover and interior design by Marissa Raybuck.

Library of Congress Control Number: 2019934245

ISBNs: 978-0-7624-9685-3 (hardcover),
978-0-7624-9687-7 (ebook)

LSC-C

10 9 8 7 6 5 4 3 2 1

TO KAITLYN, AARON, TAYLOR,
HAYLEY, BRAYDON, AND AVERY

CHAPTER ONE

I STOOD IN THE middle of the newsroom, trying to ignore the fact that it was actually my neighbor Thom's barn.

"Listen, everyone! Let's hash out the first issue," I said.

Thom smiled at me. I did not smile back. I needed to look serious. At least I had sounded serious. I had practiced calling the meeting to order in front of the bathroom mirror all morning. The trick was to square up your face so your eyes felt like pried-open windows. Next, you had to make your voice a rumble, like it started down in your toes and was being forced out of the grout stopping up your mouth.

"What's wrong with your voice?" asked my other neighbor, Min Kim-Franklin. She didn't look up from where she was adding her name to the sign-in sheet by the open barn doors.

"Nothing," I said. I looked down at her name and shuddered. I didn't like a lot about Min Kim-Franklin, but what I liked the least of all was her tendency to sign her name with a heart instead of a dot over the *i*'s.

"Something is wrong with your voice, I'm sure of it," she said. Min's only a year younger than me, but the word *baby* flashed across my mind every time I saw her. Maybe it was the ruffles. The headband holding back her smooth dark hair had little cream-colored ruffles. They matched the cream-colored blouse, also with ruffles, and her orange shorts, which had— you guessed it—ruffles running across the trim. "Are you getting a cold?" she asked.

"No," I barked.

"There, that's it again." Min pointed at me. "Your voice is all gruff and mean sounding. Maybe you should clear your throat."

"Maybe *you* should take journalism more seriously," I snapped.

"That's better." She skipped—for real—toward the back of the barn.

Thom and I had put up the flyers in the library, at Wells Diner, and in the ice cream shop announcing the formation of a newspaper club in Thom's barn. A part of me hadn't wanted Min to find out, but of course she had. Min always found out.

No time to think of that now. I had a newspaper to run. I looked across the rest of the sign-in sheet. It'd be a bare-bones staff to start, but that was true for most modern newsrooms.

All these thoughts rumbled through my mind in the same grout-mouth voice, which was a lot like my dad's when he was on super deadline. Or when I was in trouble, like that time back when we lived in the city and the family in the apartment next to ours lost their pet snake. I had sifted a very thin coat of flour across the entire kitchen floor to see if we'd have any tracks.

First on the sign-up list should've been Thom Hunter, since we were meeting in his barn. Thom lived across the street from me, and both of his parents worked from home, so they had super wi-fi connectivity that stretched right out to the barn. My new house, on the other hand, only got wi-fi in the attic bedroom, where my mom was all of the time, writing a novel or turning into a bat, whichever happened first.

Yet Thom hadn't signed in. I sighed as I watched him wander around the barn. His long floppy blond hair fell nearly across his eyes as he bent over, picked up a greenish strand of hay, and sniffed it. Then he stuffed the hay into a plastic baggie. Also in the baggie were what looked like half of a red crayon, a purple ribbon, a sprig of catnip, and a long, black feather.

I cleared my throat. "Are you ready for me to call the meeting to order?"

"Yeah, Nellie," he said. Thom's voice was the opposite of gruff. Instead, it was soft as the cotton ball I also spotted inside the bag. "I'm just adding to my bag of smells."

Thom shook the plastic baggie. I opened my mouth. Closed it. Opened it again. Closed it again. I had a meeting to run. No time to ask why he carried around a bag of smells. Thom could be a little odd, I guess. Not dot-your-*i*-with-a-heart odd, but odd in different ways. I once saw him follow a butterfly around his yard for a whole hour.

I know that sounds a little like I had been spying on Thom for an hour, which is not at all what happened. I was simply looking out my window, from which I could see only Thom's farm, and I had seized the opportunity to work on my observation skills.

I shook my head, trying to focus my thoughts on the newspaper, and stepped backward, almost onto a pile of something the goat left behind and that probably would've been a yuck addition to Thom's bag of smells. I sidestepped and cleared my throat again.

Thom settled onto a hay bale next to Min at the back of the barn. I had really hoped someone aside from Thom and Min would show up. Just then I heard rustling near the front of the barn.

"Um, hey," called out Gloria Wells, the twelve-year-old daughter of the diner owner in downtown Bear Creek. She was a year older and way cooler than me, and I was so happy to see her I could've hugged her if I was the kind of person to give people hugs (which I am *not*).

Gloria looked a lot shorter when she wasn't behind the counter of the diner, where she usually perched by the cash register. She stood on her tiptoes and peered toward the back of the barn. "Hello? I'm not sure I'm at the right place. I wanted to, um, write . . ."

"Yes," I answered. Gloria smiled when she saw me, a smile that vanished when she spotted the goat droppings. "This is the right place."

Min shot me another eyebrow-popped-up look at my grout voice. Gloria's eyes widened, too. Maybe I was overdoing it a little. "Come on in," I added a little softer.

Gloria strode past me. As she walked, some of her usual confidence snapped back into place. Leaning against the barn wall, she lifted her chin and smiled at Thom. Her forehead wrinkled when she saw his bag of smells. Thom's cheeks turned a little pink as he smiled back at her. Gloria's really pretty, with brown skin and darker eyes and soft curly hair that's even deeper brown. I grinned when I saw the notebook poking out of Gloria's shoulder bag.

I felt a little silly when I realized I was bouncing on the balls of my feet, but then I remembered Dad doing the same thing every time I saw him address his newspaper staff about a cool new project or some breaking news. And what could be more exciting than kicking off a brand-new newspaper—one that we would create entirely on our own?

We had nearly everything we needed to do just that, especially now that Gloria was here. Thom had already told me he wanted to be a writer, too. And Min, despite the hearts fascination, was a pretty incredible artist. I bet she would take on the design of the paper. The only thing missing was a photographer.

"Sorry, I'm late." I whipped around and this time didn't hold back on the toe bouncing. Because there in front of me was Gordon Burke, twelve years old like Gloria, son of the

Bear Creek School District superintendent—which meant he had handy neighborhood connections—and, best of all, a photographer. A real camera swung from a strap around his neck. "I'm not too sure I really want to do the whole newspaper thing," he said, scratching the back of his neck where the harness probably rubbed against his skin. "But I thought . . ."

"Come in! Come in!" I clapped my hands. "Okay, everybody. Let's get planning."

"Wait," Gordon said. He leaned backward, peeking around the side of the barn. "Are you coming?"

Stepping forward, head hanging low with a curtain of red hair falling around her face, was a girl I had spotted when I stopped to hang up a flyer at Wells Diner. "I'm, um, Charlotte," she whispered.

Copy editor. I immediately pegged her.

And that's how the Newspaper Club came together, right in Thom Hunter's old barn. But maybe I'm burying the **lede** a little. That's what Dad calls it when a reporter puts the most interesting part about an article down in the middle or toward the end.

Maybe I should start at the beginning.

CHAPTER TWO

STARTING A STORY DOESN'T take a lot of creativity.

That's what Dad tells me all the time. He says it's easy to spot **cub reporters** (*cub* means "new" in newspaper speak) because their articles are trying too hard.

Good stories have to answer just five questions: *Who? What? When? Where?* and *Why?*

"People pick up a paper because they want the news, and your job as a reporter is to give it to them as quickly and clearly as possible," Dad says. "Don't make it complicated for the reader. Just lay the story out there."

Most of the time, reporters have to answer all five of those questions in one paragraph. Before I even dreamed of the Newspaper Club, I thought this would be how an article about my life in Bear Creek would begin:

> Nellie Murrow, 11 years old, is spending her first month of summer break before becoming a fifth grader at Bear Creek Park hiding from her nemesis, Min Kim-Franklin.

Min is the reason I was festering away in little Bear Creek, Maine, instead of enjoying the city, where there are proper parks, with way more slides and swings and climbing walls, and especially way more kids and fewer squawky birds and huge trees.

Min. She's responsible for all of my heartache. The reason I'm in a town with only one diner, one gas station, and, worst of all, only *one* newspaper. Everyone knows the best towns are two-newspaper towns—where every reporter has to fight to be first to share breaking news. ("Nothing motivates a journalist like a **scoop**," Dad said. I mean, *says*. I haven't actually spoken with him in a few days.)

While we're being technical, I guess it wasn't *really* Min's fault that such a fate has befallen me. Really, it was her mom's fault. Min's mom, Mrs. Kim-Franklin, is my mom's best friend from college. They were sorority sisters and always did the super-secret sorority handshake when they saw each other, even though now we're neighbors and we (unfortunately) see the Kim-Franklins every stinking day. When the newspaper where my parents worked—Mom on the crime **beat** and Dad as the news director—folded six months after Dad left for a new marketing job in Asia, Mom called Mrs. Kim-Franklin crying.

Mrs. Kim-Franklin went ahead and ruined our lives by talking about the old farmhouse for sale next door to her house and how amazing it was to raise Min in Bear Creek. Then she threw in that Min could be my very best friend in the whole world, just like she and Mom were best friends. The next thing you know, Mom was having huddled phone conversations in the pantry behind the closed door. And *then?* We bought an ugly farmhouse without even seeing it, and Mom announced that she was going to take a year "sabbatical," which meant holing up in her attic office and writing a novel.

I couldn't even complain to Dad about it, not when he was at a job with a firm in Asia. I was betting he'd come back later this summer. He had to spend a few months immersed in the culture at the firm, but I was sure he'd start telecommuting next year.

All I could say was, this was *not* the family that raised me. Working for corporations? Writing a novel? Puke and double puke.

Everyone else changed, but I stayed the same.

And I wasn't about to be assigned a new best friend. It was bad enough being the kid who always ate lunch alone or spent it talking to a teacher. I *knew* other people made friends easily. But having to endure my summer knowing Min was required to spend time with me was too much to bear. I knew that's what was behind her trailing me all the time. If it weren't for her mom and my mom forcing it, I was sure Min would be like everyone else and leave me alone.

Not that I cared.

Mrs. Kim-Franklin watched over every single thing Min did as if at any moment she could burst into flames or break out in hives. I was accustomed to a certain amount of freedom. Mom used to say I was her free-range city kid. I even had my own subway pass!

But Min wasn't allowed to go exploring, not without her mom lagging behind us. All summer my plan was: slip out of the house first thing in the morning and get to the park alone. Then I could slouch on the swing and hear myself think without Min's chirp-chirp-chirping.

The swings at the park were the only thing I liked about Bear Creek. Maybe everything else was different, but the playground swings were just the same as the ones Dad used to push me on back in the city.

Dad and I used to go to the park right outside our garden district apartment every single day of the summer. Dad had worked at the newspaper in the evening, so we went first thing in the morning. Hardly anyone was there, or maybe they just knew the swings were for us, because we always had the two on the end ready and waiting. After giving me a few good pushes, he'd sit in the swing next to me and we'd compete to see who could go the highest. Eventually, though, we'd both stop pumping our legs and just be there next to each other. We talked a lot, me and my dad. Or, at least, we used to.

It was sometimes hard to reach him now. Kind of funny, isn't it, that the swings were the only place in Bear Creek with good enough reception for me to reach Dad? We have had the best conversations on those swings. Maybe you'd think it'd be scary to talk with someone while flying higher than probably anyone ever has in Bear Creek. But it wasn't scary for me.

I liked to pump my legs until I was soaring so high, I was just about horizontal to the ground. I didn't see anything down there, not one bit of Bear Creek. That's how I liked it. Plus, there was always one second when my body lifted straight up off the rubber seat and the only thing keeping me on Earth was the metal loops of the chain in each hand. And I wasn't even scared.

Maybe that's because I'm named after **Nellie Bly**. She was the bravest person. Nellie Bly once traveled around the whole world in seventy-two days just to get a story. Another time, she heard that people sent to institutions were being mistreated there. She wanted the scoop, so she pretended to be a patient in order to be sent to an institution, even though it meant being abused. She did whatever it took to get the story and share the truth.

Journalists have to be brave. I know this because I've lived my whole life in a newsroom, thanks to my parents. My mom is super brave. Before her sabbatical, she'd step right up to the yellow caution tape at crime scenes so she could interview police or **sources** (that's newspaper speak for someone who can provide information **on the record**. "On the record" means the source says it's okay to print what they say).

Once, Mom was filling in for a features reporter, covering a story about a new skydiving place. The company offered to give her the real experience so she could write her story with authenticity. Mom and the photojournalist she was working with each strapped on parachute vests. And then she jumped right out of an airplane, her arms spread wide like she was leaping into a ball pit. The photojournalist snapped a shot of that moment and sent it to my dad, who, for Christmas that year, gave Mom a framed portrait of the photo. We hung it in the dining room. But that was in our city apartment. I'm not sure where the picture is now, probably in one of the dozens of boxes stacked on top of the table.

Loads of times I've helped Mom write her stories or helped Dad edit other stories. I was a journalist, too, even though my stories hadn't been published yet. I guess, technically, I was still a cub.

But now Mom wouldn't even let me read the novel she was working on. She said it was inappropriate. And who knew if Dad was even able to write at his new job? Bleh.

Maybe if I could reach him, I'd ask him if he'd written anything. That's what was most important about the park being a Min-free zone. I could sit on the swings alone and really talk to Dad without feeling like I was being babysat by someone younger than me who still wore ruffles. And, technically, Dad and I were both starting our day talking with each other, since ten in the morning in Bear Creek was midnight in Tokyo. Dad didn't mind my calling him at midnight because he was a night owl.

But this particular morning's conversation with Dad hadn't gone as well as I wanted. He kept whispering ridiculous things, such as "give Bear Creek a chance" and "take it easy on your mother; she's been through a lot," and even "I'm sure Min's not that bad. Even if she *has* to spend time with you, that doesn't mean you should be mean to her."

Every day he spent away from us, Dad became less of the hard-nosed, facts-only journalist I knew and more of a stranger. Sometimes I even had a hard time remembering his crinkly-eyed smile when I'd walk into the newsroom after school. I tried not to think about that while I worked on swinging higher than I had yesterday. When I got really, really high, the swing set would hop and I'd get a little bounce off the seat.

I bet Nellie Bly wouldn't blink when that happened either.

The only problem with soaring into the sky on a swing is sometimes you need to get back to the ground fast without breaking your legs.

That was the predicament I found myself in when the screaming started. When I first heard the screeching, I thought it was one of the black birds swooping through the bright blue patch of sky over me. But then the shriek ended in a definitely human word I'm not allowed to say out loud.

As the swing fell back toward land, I dragged my feet, the heels of my sneakers sending up a cloud of dry dirt around me. It took a couple more back-and-forths before the swing slowed enough that I could jump and not crumple into a broken-bones pile. I still fell forward onto my knees. One of them even bled a little bit when I squeezed the skin together. It took some time to limp over to where the screeching had started.

Bear Creek was such a boring ole stick-in-the-mud town that Police Chief Rodgers beat me to the scene.

If Chief Rodgers were a mannequin at the mall (not that Bear Creek *had* a mall), he'd topple over. His legs, even in his uniform's dark brown pants, were stick skinny, but his belly was as wide as our washing machine. Sort of shaped the same way, too. His head was normal sized but a bushy brown mustache stretched out to the sides.

I could see the ends of that mustache twitching up and down, up and down as he talked with the source of all the screeching. Peeking around Chief Rodgers, I pulled my notebook out. Even cub reporters like me know to always have a notebook and two pens in their back pocket. I scribbled down notes. At the top I wrote, *WHO?* Under it: *Middle-aged man. Fluffy white hair. Angry face.*

"I'm telling you, Chief," the man said. "I was attacked!"

"Attacked?" Twitch, twitch went the chief's mustache. "By who, exactly?"

Whom, I corrected, but only in my head. (Mom says, though it's great to understand grammar—an important tool in every writer's toolbox—it's better to keep edits to yourself, especially when talking with grown-ups.)

"I don't know!" the man bellowed. His hat, a baseball cap, was scrunched up in his fist. He swung it up and then hit his thigh with it. "If I knew that, I wouldn't be calling you, would I?"

Twitch, twitch went Chief Rodgers's mustache. "All right, Hank. Settle down." *Hank,* I wrote in my notebook. "Take me through it one more time."

Hank's watery brown eyes shifted around the park. I glanced around, too. A couple walking their dog seemed to slow as they passed by, clearly listening in. I couldn't blame them; nothing new happened in Bear Creek.

Hank drew in a big breath, making his shoulders peak. "I told you. I was walking to my truck. I just had a cup of coffee from Wells Diner and needed to use the facilities." The hand not holding his hat jerked toward the brick building for men's and women's bathrooms behind him. "Then I'm walking back, you see. And *bam!* Someone attacked me!"

"What exactly did they do, Hank?" I asked.

Both Hank and Chief Rodgers paused. Their mouths popped open a little as they turned toward me. Chief Rodgers's jaw clenched. Hank closed his mouth. They looked at each other. Figures. So many people ignore the power of the press.

As if I hadn't spoken, Chief Rodgers said, "Hank, what exactly happened?"

Hank swallowed. "Someone swiped my hat right off my head!"

"The hat in your hand?" I asked.

Again, the men looked at me. Chief Rodgers cleared his throat. "Why don't you go play and let me handle this, kid?" I didn't move. The **First Amendment** offers freedom to the press. Chief Rodgers turned back to Hank. "The hat in your hand?" he asked.

"Yeah. They swiped it right off my head. I fell forward, smack on my knees." I lifted my own sort-of bloody knee in empathy, but Hank ignored me. "I spilled my coffee!" Hank yanked out his T-shirt, which had a dark splotch all down the front. "Yelled something right in my ear, too!"

"What did they yell?" Chief Rodgers and I asked at the same time. I smiled at him and gave a little nod so he'd know he was doing a good job with the questioning. He rolled his eyes.

"I don't know, man!" Hank said. "I was too busy falling over!"

Chief Rodgers crossed his arms. "Did you see anyone in the bathroom when you were there?"

Hank shook his head.

"What about anyone at the park as you walked in?"

"Just this girl on the swings."

Chief Rodgers glanced at me. One of his eyebrows popped up like a tent. "Did you see anyone, kid?"

I shook my head. "I was looking mostly at the sky. That's how high I was making the swing go."

Chief Rodgers didn't look impressed. He must not have seen me. "Well, there aren't any footprints in the dirt. No witnesses. Is it possible you tripped?" Chief Rodgers asked.

"Tripped?" Hank gasped. "'Course I didn't *trip*. C'mon, now. I'm telling you—I was *attacked*."

A gasp behind me made Chief Rodgers whip around so fast he had to grip his neck afterward. In front of me, Hank nodded vigorously. I didn't bother to turn. I just sighed. I knew that gasp.

Mrs. Kim-Franklin. And that meant Min had found me. Great.

And just when Bear Creek was starting to get interesting.

CHAPTER THREE

"ATTACKED?" MRS. KIM-FRANKLIN ECHOED. She grabbed Min's shoulder, pulling her close, as if Min had been about to dart ahead right into the alleged attacker.

And maybe she would've because Min is a baby. Technically, she's a fourth grader. I remember those days. Back when life was easy and I wasn't the only one who could do math in my head.

I don't think *all* fourth graders are babies. I certainly wasn't a baby last year when I was a fourth grader. But Min is one. Maybe it's the way that she's always smiling, her cute little dimples showing, one on each cheek. Maybe it's the way she always looks like someone's about to hand her an ice cream cone. Maybe—and this is the worst thing of all—maybe it's the way she dots the *i* in her name with a heart. A heart!

Min and I are nothing alike. Nothing. Even so, she keeps calling me her best friend. I knew her mom was making her be nice to me, but even when Mrs. Kim-Franklin wasn't around—even when it was just the two of us—Min would find a way to say that I was her best friend. And since I didn't know anyone else in Bear Creek (and, okay, since I didn't really have any friends my age in the city where I used to live) I guess she technically *was* my best friend, too, just by nature of her being my only friend. It was a pickle.

"If people are being attacked at the park, the public needs to know," said Mrs. Kim-Franklin.

"Now, now," Chief Rodgers said. "Hank here claims something knocked him—"

"I was attacked!" Hank interrupted.

"Hold up," Chief Rodgers continued. "Don't jump to conclusions here. Who would want to attack you?"

"Well, until you get to the bottom of it," Mrs. Kim-Franklin said, "my girls will be staying home."

I realized with horror that she meant me, too. I was one of her girls. How had I become one of her girls? Was *I* going to dot my *i* with a heart soon? What would become of me?

When we first moved here, Mrs. Kim-Franklin had said that everyone took care of each other in Bear Creek, and I guess that meant I was now one of her girls. *Gah!* Mrs. Kim-Franklin was as much like my mom as I was like Min, which is to say not at all.

Mrs. Kim-Franklin was wearing a crisp white sundress with a bright red belt across her small waist. Her blond hair was swept back into a ponytail at the crown of her head. Her lips were the same red as the belt, as were her sandals. When we arrived in Bear Creek, Mom had hugged her and said, "Sandra, you haven't changed a bit! You still look like the sorority queen."

Mrs. Kim-Franklin's eyes had drifted down Mom, taking in her messy hair and old band T-shirt. She said, "You haven't changed, either, Wendy!"

Though Min always dressed in fancy clothes like her mom, she physically looked more like her dad, who was Korean. Min has his hair and complexion. (Fact: *Franklin* was actually Mrs. Kim-Franklin's maiden name; she said "Franklin-Kim" just didn't have the right ring to it.) Today, Min was wearing a white T-shirt with fluffy ruffles and red-and-white checked shorts. Her socks had the same little ruffle as her shirt. The Kim-Franklins were big on ruffles.

Mrs. Kim-Franklin opened her mouth and I just knew she was about to ruin my life with whatever no-more-park-for-my-girls nonsense she was about to say.

"So," I said to Chief Rodgers in my best reporter voice (serious and factual). I tapped the notebook with my pen as I consulted my notes. "We don't have any witnesses. We don't have a motive. We don't have a description. What we have seems to be a misunderstanding. Page three material, really."

None of the adults said anything. I felt their eyes burning into the top of my head, so I stared at the notebook. A plop of water out of nowhere fell onto the page, rolled down, and blurred my ink marks.

"It's beginning to drizzle," Mrs. Kim-Franklin said, "so it's not as though it's a good park day, anyway. Nellie, we'll give you a ride home."

"Or . . ." Min said, "we could play as fast as we can until it actually rains!" She grabbed my arm and ducked us out of the trio of adults and toward the slides.

Sometimes Min's all right, I guess.

"Hold on!" Mrs. Kim-Franklin called out.

"It's hardly even sprinkling," Min whined. She sprinted ahead to be first on the slide ladder. I was fast on her heels. As we ran past, a cluster of jet-black birds took to the sky.

That's when Hank's page-three story became **top-of-the-fold** material.

"Chief Rodgers!" someone yelled from the parking lot. A young couple trotted toward the chief, Mrs. Kim-Franklin, and Hank. "Hey, Chief!"

I shushed Min, who was busy singing about being top of the slide. ("I'm the slide, slide, *slide*. Top of the slide. And you're. At. The. Bottom." Oh, Min. If I *wanted* to, I totally could've beat you to the slide. I chose not to, Min. I chose not to.)

Min silently slid to the bottom. "Something's going down," I whispered as she popped up.

"Yeah, it was me. Just now," Min whispered back.

I rolled my eyes and motioned to the cluster of adults. I pressed a finger against my lips. Slowly, we crept up on the group. I tried to stay squarely behind Chief Rodgers's barrel chest.

But Min? She took superlong steps like a cartoon spy, her finger pressed to her lips the whole time.

The woman straightened when she saw us coming up behind the chief. Her arms crossed and eyes narrowed with suspicion.

I resented the glare. Quietly moving toward my sources as they discussed something in a public space was a totally legitimate journalistic practice. "I think some kids are messing with us," the woman said. She nudged the man beside her, and soon he, too, stood with crossed arms, glaring at Min and me.

Chief Rodgers sighed. "What now?"

"Our wipers aren't working," the man said.

"Now why would that be kids' doing?" The chief mumbled something under his breath about everybody making assumptions.

"They're not working because the rubber strip was ripped out of them." The woman tilted her head in my direction again, her eyes boring into my pockets.

I rolled my eyes, held the notebook under my chin, and emptied my pockets. Nothing but rocks were inside. I like shiny rocks.

The man gestured to his car. The wiper blades were standing up like broken arms. I squinted at them as I righted my notebook. "What would a kid want with wiper rubber?"

"I don't know, kid," the woman said. "You tell me."

"Are you accusing my girls of stealing?" Mrs. Kim-Franklin leaned toward the couple. Her finger jutted out. "I'll have you know that I *watch* my girls. They would *never—*"

"It's my attacker!" Hank cut in. "I told you! Ha! I told you I was attacked. Ha!"

"Look," Chief Rodgers said with a sigh that began down at his stick legs, rattled around his barrel belly, and poofed out from his mouth. "Just because Hank here thinks something might've happened to knock him upside the head and your wipers are deficient does *not* mean anything illegal took place. We haven't had rain in two, three weeks. How do you know something happened to your wipers today at the park?"

"Good question," I whispered to Chief Rodgers, who totally didn't appreciate the compliment. He just puffed out a smaller sigh.

"Because my sunglasses are missing, too," the man said. "I had them on the dash of the car. When it started to rain, I remembered that I had left the window open and we ran back to the car. They're gone."

Chief Rodgers scribbled something in his notebook while the woman elbowed the man's side. "How many times have I told you to make sure your windows are closed! Those were expensive glasses!"

"I told you!" Hank shouted and jabbed his finger up at the sky. "Someone knocked me down. Stole his glasses! Stole his wiper blade stuff! They are probably trying to fashion a disguise or something."

Chief Rodgers's mustache twitched something fierce.

"All circumstantial," I said. Chief nodded.

But just then my park-going independent life was once again compromised. "Chief Rodgers!" yelped someone else from the parking lot. We all turned toward the new source, an older woman holding a pink umbrella beside her equally pink car. "Someone stole my car keys! I left them on that bench while I used the restroom, and now they're gone!"

"Did you check your purse?" Chief Rodgers asked.

"Of course I checked my purse. I'm telling you, they were right there!" She pointed to the bench, empty except for a couple crows hopping around its base.

"Like I said," said Hank, throwing his arm toward the woman in pink. "Knocked me down. Disguised themselves. Then tried to get away, like, with a stolen car."

"The car's still there." Chief Rodgers pointed to the pink car.

"Well, yeah. Once they saw the car, they changed their mind."

Chief Rodgers sighed again as the couple, the woman in pink, Hank, and Mrs. Kim-Franklin all began speaking at once. He reached into his back pocket and pulled out his note-book again. I stood on my tiptoes to see what he scribbled across the page. *Vandalism, possible theft, at the park.*

"C'mon, girls," Mrs. Kim-Franklin said and put a hand on each of our shoulders. "This isn't a place for children."

"It's a *park*!" I cried.

But Mrs. Kim-Franklin just shepherded us to her gold minivan. I knew better than to argue with a get-in-the-car mom face.

When we got back to her house, Min asked, "Want to come in and play with my dolls?"

Dad says it's important to provide visual clues to readers. So, here's what you'd see from Mrs. Kim-Franklin's gold minivan as she parked in front of her house: a bright white two-story house with black shutters and a shiny red door; three bushes clipped into little mounds on each side of the front step; a perfectly symmetrical tree in the middle of dazzling green grass; a white picket fence around the house and yard.

Then, if you looked to the right, you'd see our house.

Picture a farmhouse that is mostly straight and square, with a rectangular section that pops out of the side. Once upon a time, probably back when it was built a hundred years ago, it must've been as bright white as Min's house. But I was pretty sure it hadn't been painted since the day it was made, so now it is kind of grayish. The front door is also gray. There is a gigantic rosebush by the front door with sunshine yellow blossoms. On our first morning in Bear Creek it had snagged Mrs. Kim-Franklin's sweater as she walked into the house with a basket full of muffins. She said it should be trimmed back into an orderly hedge.

I loved the rosebush just the way it was.

"Nellie?" Min prodded again.

"No, I don't play with dolls," I said.

"What about the box under your bed?" she asked.

I whipped around. "What did you just say?"

"The box of dolls under your bed?" Min replied and, for some reason, twirled around in a circle.

"How do you know about that?"

Min shrugged. "Your mom said I could play with your dolls when I was bored last time I was over. Remember? You stayed in the bathroom the whole visit, ignoring your very best friend in the whole world."

"Those are *not* dolls," I snapped, momentarily regretting my decision to lock the door and read in the bathroom when Min had stopped by. "Those are story devices. I use them to act out stories when I'm stuck. So I can offer better physical descriptions. That's *it*. It isn't *play*."

"Why do you have so many hairbrushes and ribbons then? And little outfits?" Min crossed her arms, looking a lot like her mom.

"For *reenactments*." I marched toward my house. How dare she imply that I played with dolls.

"Why do you make them dance or hold them out like this"—she held her arms straight out like she was holding an imaginary doll between them—"while you dance?"

I stomped. *"That* never happened! And you better stop staring into my room!" Unfortunately, Min's bedroom window faces *my* bedroom window.

Min just smiled. When she smiled like that, I could see the heart dotting the *i* in her name. I stomped all the way home.

———————————

"I'm home!" I called up the stairs. "Breaking news! Something is going down at the park!"

I paused on the second step next to a cracked-open box of kitchen supplies. Mom's style of unpacking seemed to be mostly find-what-you-need-and-leave-the-rest. The whole house was sprinkled with half-empty boxes.

I stood there, waiting. If Mom was having a bad writing day, she'd answer within five seconds. And her answer would actually apply to what she had just heard. If she was having a good writing day, it'd take about a minute for the words I'd said to push past the ones she was lacing together for her story. But even then, she wouldn't totally have heard what I said, her mind clouded by what she was imagining, so the reply would be something totally unrelated.

She hadn't always been like that. She used to talk out her stories with me, telling me all about why she had decided to put some information up higher and other details toward the bottom of the article she was working on. But that was when she had been writing news stories, not a whole novel.

It also had been when Dad was still around. A lot had changed since he left. Sometimes I felt like everything had changed. The only time things felt *right* was when I was on those swings. I kicked one of the boxes in the hall; maybe Mom had accidentally packed up her usual self inside one.

I watched my phone. A minute passed. Thirty more seconds. Then, "Hi, Nellie! Yes, soup for dinner tonight!"

I sighed. It had been a good writing day. That hadn't happened in a while, so I couldn't be too upset. But I really wanted to hash out what could be going on at the park with a seasoned reporter like her. I thumbed through my contacts, my finger hovering over Dad's info. I pushed the phone back in my pocket.

Sometimes you've got to scout out your sources through the back door. That was another of Dad's sayings. He didn't mean actually showing up at people's back door, though. Fact: That could get a person arrested. No, he meant that if you couldn't speak directly to a source, you should be clever about it. Find a different way to get to the information you needed.

What I needed was to know more about Bear Creek Park. The best way would be to talk to a town expert—a reporter in Bear Creek. Mom had started a local newspaper subscription the day we moved to town, but I hadn't been impressed with the coverage. Mostly it seemed to focus on spaghetti suppers at the Episcopalian church. I also hadn't figured out where the newsroom was located. Most likely downtown.

Music drifted from the house across the street and in our open living room window. I squatted on the stairs so I could see through the curtains to the road. A boy my age named Thom lived there; I had seen him walking from the big brown barn in his backyard to his rambling blue house. Strings of yellow lights lit the path between the two. The barn looked as run-down as my house, but the house was robin-egg cheery. There were patchwork-like flowers blooming in all different colors in window boxes under every window. When we first pulled into our driveway in the moving truck, I had hopped out of the car and jumped up and down. "I love it!" I had said, thinking Thom's house was ours. Mrs. Kim-Franklin (of course she had been waiting for us in the driveway) had crossed her arms when my face crumpled as I realized my mistake. She calls Thom's home an "unorthodox Colonial." But the jutting-out sections and the windows of all different sizes are what I loved most about it—it reminded me of when Dad would call out to a reporter that he had a few more inches to fill on the page, meaning the reporter could go into more detail. Almost always the reporter would do a little wiggle or fist pump, excited to tack on to the story.

I stared at the house again. Okay, so I liked Thom's house. But actually going over there and talking to Thom? And his moms? I filled up my lungs.

Another of Dad's sayings trickled through my mind along with the country music from across the street. This one wasn't about being a reporter. It was about being a friend. *You've got to put yourself out there, Nellie.*

Not that making friends was *scary.* It was just not something I enjoyed. Being around someone my age usually ended with me trying over and over again to come up with something to say next before finally asking where the kid's parents were and hanging out with them until my parents could come get me.

I liked the idea of friends, of course, but when I was around a lot of people my age, I found that I'd rather be by myself—most of the time. My heart squished a little. The truth was, maybe I *did* want to have a friend, a real friend, one that I made myself. I turned back to the stairs, knocking the boxes.

Being brave doesn't mean you aren't scared, Nellie. It means you can be scared and do what you need to do anyway.

"Mom!" I called up the stairs. "I'm going over to Thom's house."

It wasn't like I was going to go over there *just* to make a friend. Or hang out in a cozy house. I had a story to scout.

Mom's voice floated down the stairs. "M'kay."

CHAPTER FOUR

I EASED OPEN THE back door and gently pulled it shut behind me. Then I flattened myself against the side of the house until I was on the far side, away from Min's house. At the front of the house, pressed once again to its side, I checked to see if I could spot any movement from the Kim-Franklin house, being sure to check the third-floor window that overlooked the yard. She was always looking, that Min.

Satisfied, I darted across the street.

I stood by a huge oak tree in Thom's side yard. The barn was in front of me, and I could smell the hay his moms kept there for the goat. I could also smell the goat. A black cat threaded between my legs while I stood there. I figured Thom was in the barn because I had spotted him walking in that direction while I was inside my house, but I didn't know whether to go straight there. It'd be like admitting I was going all Min-like and spying on him, when really, I had just been staring out my window and happened to notice him.

Plus, the music coming from his house wasn't awful. And the longer I stood there, the more I heard—like one of his moms telling a story and the other laughing. I also smelled a roast beef dinner. I hadn't had a roast beef dinner in a long time. I licked my lips, considering what to do.

"Which way you gonna go?" The voice drifted down from above.

"*God?*" I gasped.

Just then something dropped down from the tree. Thom.

He was eleven years old, just like me, but much taller. Skinnier, too. His honey-colored hair flew up as he fell and then flopped back over his forehead to where his dark eyelashes mixed with his bangs. He was wearing jeans that looked like he had cut them into shorts while wearing them. His T-shirt was covered in old paint splotches. I realized he was watching me as closely as I was him. I glanced down to see what he was seeing—my gray shorts, black T-shirt, gray sneakers. I liked the monotone look.

As Thom continued to stare at me, I realized he was waiting for an answer to his question. "Oh, I just have a couple questions, you know."

"I don't know," Thom said.

"What were you doing up there?" I asked and pointed at the tree. It was dusk, and under the tree canopy, it was already shadowy.

"That's what you came over to ask?" Thom replied.

"I thought you were in your barn," I said.

This time, Thom was the one who took too long to respond. "I'm not," he finally said.

"Yeah, I know," I said.

"Did you come over to see if I was in my barn?" Thom's eyebrow popped up under his shaggy hair.

"No."

He stared at me.

"I'm, um, here to find out some information."

"Thom!" called a voice from the house. "Time for dinner."

"Coming!" he answered.

"I'll stop by another time," I said, then dragged in a big roast beef breath.

"Why don't you come for dinner?" Thom turned back to the house. "Ma! Can a friend come for dinner?" he shouted before I could answer. Maybe he knew it would take me a while. Wait. *Was I* a friend? I bit the inside of my cheek to keep from asking out loud.

"Of course!" his mom shouted. The back door, painted magenta, flew open. "Come on, guys! Thom, I need you to whip the potatoes."

"Are you coming?" Thom asked. By the time he turned back to me, I already was texting Mom that she could have all the soup; I was going to have roast beef at Thom's house.

When Mom, Dad, and I had dinner together, it had always been pretty quiet. Mom would tell us about whatever story she was working on. Dad would complain about whoever kept forgetting to refill the coffeepot. I'd tell them about school.

Luckily, we almost never had dinner at home except on weekends. Dad would work all evening to make sure the stories were edited and laid out for the morning paper, so usually Mom and I would walk the two blocks from our apartment to the newsroom and have dinner with Dad there. Once Mom even brought a hot plate so my dad could make scrambled eggs and pancakes, and we could have Mom's favorite—Breakfast for Dinner. Everyone, from the night janitor to the lifestyle reporter to the police beat, dunked pancakes in syrup and shouted over each other about what they were working on for deadline.

The best was when they jockeyed for more space, each of them arguing why they deserved more room for features or investigative pieces. No, that's not right. The *best* was when they'd talk about people calling in with "tips," such as this one lady who called in every day to report that her neighbor's yard horse was infringing on existing livestock laws. (When the intern went to dig into the story, she discovered that the yard horse was actually made of cement and when the old man who owned it heard about the complaints, he started decorating it for the holidays. He sent a Christmas card in to the paper the next year—the yard horse was wearing an elf hat and had a red sparkly nose.)

Mom would smile and laugh with everyone as Dad flipped pancakes onto paper plates, and everyone would listen when I asked questions. "Hey, hey!" The police beat would call out if they didn't. "Little Cub here needs to be heard."

After we ate, I'd sit beside Dad at the news desk and do my homework while Mom made calls for whatever story she was working on. The half dozen televisions in the newsroom would all be tuned to different stations. The police scanner was next to me on Dad's desk. The air smelled like old pizza, stale coffee, and newsprint. Sometimes other reporters' or editors' kids would hang out in the newsroom, too, but usually I was the only cub.

On really special days—such as election night—Mom and I would be at the newsroom all night, right up until the paper went to press at midnight.

I realized how much I missed the newsroom's buzzing and movement and laughter as I stood in an orange halo of light outside Thom's back door. Beside me, Thom pointed to his mother dancing to the music in front of the stove, where she was whisking gravy. Her long silver hair hung in a heavy braid down the middle of her back. When she turned to the side, I saw she was wearing bold red lipstick and dark black eyeliner. "That's Ma," he said. "You can call her Sheila. That's what Gerald did."

"Who's Gerald?" I asked.

Thom stared at his feet a second before answering. "He was my best friend." Thom rubbed at his chest. "He lived in your house. He's gone now."

I felt my eyes bugging. "I *thought* the house could be haunted! I mean, look at it!" I yelped, thumbing to my house behind me.

Thom's eyes scrunched. "Why would it be haunted?"

"You said he's gone now. Like, Gerald is no longer . . ."

Thom's laughter puffed out of his nose. It took about five puffs before I even realized he was laughing. "Gerald isn't *dead*. He moved to Atlanta."

"Oh," I said.

"I don't think your house is haunted. I think it's just waiting," he said.

"Waiting?" I repeated.

He nodded. "For you and your mom. To make it something really cool."

I had only talked with Thom a couple times. Every time he said things that made my thoughts wrinkle. I concentrated on the vibrant color streaming from his kitchen as I tried to smooth them out. "Your house looks warm." Then my cheeks felt warm at saying something so dorky.

The music switched from country to an eighties band. A different woman sashayed into the kitchen. She carried a tray of salad dressings in one hand. In the other, she held up her phone. "How about this one? Look, he's so small!" She said the word like *smol*.

"We don't need another goat. They stink," Sheila said. "Let's get some chickens."

"Like chickens don't stink!" The woman laughed.

Thom's chin jerked in her direction. "That's my mom. Gerald called her by her first name—Melanie. You can do that, too."

Would they like me as much as they liked Gerald? Thom smiled at me. "My moms like everyone," he said, totally reading my mind.

"Hi there!" Melanie dropped the tray and her phone on the table and clapped her hands. She was wearing an apron with softball-sized bundles of brightly colored yarn tucked inside. Crochet needles were stashed in her pulled-back dark hair. "New friends! Hurray!"

"Don't scare the newbie," Sheila said. She waved her whisk at me. "Do you like mashed potatoes?"

"Yes, ma'am," I said.

"Sheila," she replied. "Call me Sheila. All of Thom's friends do."

"You mean my one friend *did*," Thom muttered. "He moved, remember?"

Both parents paused for a moment, their smiles suddenly not as bright.

I shrugged. *Be brave,* I heard my dad say. "Well, now I'm here."

Melanie squealed and Sheila quickly turned back to the gravy, but I saw her wipe at her eyes.

We were eating dessert—bread pudding with caramel sauce—before I remembered why I had come over to Thom's house. "Vandals and thieves!" I blurted so loudly that Sheila choked for a second.

"Where?" Melanie yelped. She dropped her crochet needles into her bowl of bread pudding.

"At the park," I said. "I mean, earlier today." Quickly, I told them what had happened that morning, with Hank being shoved from behind, the rubber on the wiper blades being yanked out, and maybe even the car keys and sunglasses being lifted.

"Wiper blade rubber is such a weird thing for a thief to take," Sheila pointed out. "What could they want with that?"

Melanie shrugged and then reached across the table for more caramel sauce. "Just to be a pain, I guess."

"I don't think it makes sense either, but until someone figures out what's going on, Mrs. Kim-Franklin's going to convince Mom not to let me go to the park. And the park's the only place in Bear Creek I like!"

Sheila and Melanie exchanged a look.

"The *only* place?" Thom asked.

I felt my face burn. "Well, I mean, before I came here. Your house is great. I haven't really seen a lot of the town, I guess. Just the park, really. And my house."

They exchanged another look. "We haven't had a chance to meet your mom yet, Nellie," Sheila said.

"Mom's up in the attic writing a romance novel." I scooped another bite of bread pudding into my mouth. Despite the gross name, it's actually pretty good—a lot like what my grandma used to make and call monkey bread. "My dad's in Asia, working with a big corporation or something there. He'd be all over this story, figuring it out so we could go to the park like we used to."

"Asia?" Thom echoed. "But I thought—"

Sheila thrust the caramel sauce in his direction. "Have some more of this, Thom."

He shrugged and poured more sauce on his pudding.

"Oh," Melanie said. "Well, you're welcome here anytime. There's always a place for you at the table."

Thom stirred beside me, shuffling in his seat a little. "I could, um, I could walk with you to the newspaper tomorrow. If you want, I mean. It's right downtown."

"Really?" Suddenly Bear Creek didn't seem so miserable. I caught myself bouncing and clapping like Min tended to do. I cleared my throat. "That would be great."

CHAPTER FIVE

THE NEXT DAY—SATURDAY—I HEADED to Thom's as soon as I saw the lights come on in the Hunters' kitchen. As I crossed the street, I paused to make sure that Min wasn't peering out her window at me.

There was a difference, just so you know, between how I was watching Thom's house and how Min wouldn't let up on mine. I was watching Thom's house the way a reporter must monitor a source. Or, in this case, a source that would get me to *the* source I really needed—the newspaper. Min just watched my house because her mom told her she had to be my best friend.

I paused under the oak tree. "Hello?" I whispered, just in case.

I jumped when the voice came from behind me. "Whatcha doing?"

Min Kim-Franklin.

Today, Min was wearing a yellow sundress with, you guessed it, ruffles and a matching bow in her hair. I looked down at my outfit. Gray T-shirt. Darker gray shorts. Black sandals. No hair bow. Ever.

"I'm here to talk with Thom," I said and crossed my arms. "We have important business to discuss."

"I love important business!" Min bounced and clapped her hands.

Just then Thom opened the back door, an apple hanging from his mouth. After latching the door behind him, he pulled it from his mouth with a loud snap. "Oh, cool," he said. "You're here."

Min and I looked at each other, I guess both wondering which of us he meant. Min smiled as though it were her and skipped ahead. "Does your mom know where you are?" I asked her.

Min stopped mid-skip. Her back was to me. Super stiffly, she turned her head. I gasped when I saw her expression. For someone in ruffles, she could make her face fierce. "If you tell her, I'll suggest to Mom that you join my Gal Campers troupe." She crossed her arms. "We start each meeting holding hands and singing while we gallop in a circle."

"You *wouldn't*."

"And we have a craft hour. Lots of glitter. Even in the glue."

I shuddered. "Fine," I snapped. "You can come along."

Min smiled then turned and skipped ahead.

I sighed and trudged forward.

———————————

To get to the newspaper, we walked (or, in Min's case, skipped) about ten blocks. I guessed they were blocks, anyway. Bear Creek sort of meandered around, past a wooded area and around an old cemetery that was on the far side of the park. Min jumped when a crow cawed at us as we passed the cemetery, but Thom just called back to it with a squawk.

To get to the downtown area, we had to cross a river. Not in a hitch-the-wagon sort of way. We simply walked on the passenger side of a big metal bridge the cars went over. I tried not to be snobby about the downtown, but really? It was nothing like a proper downtown in the city. No huge lit-up billboards, cabs swerving in and out, horns honking, and people shouting.

Not one whiff of the sauerkraut and ketchup smell wafting from hotdog carts. No kids standing at cross streets with coolers of ice water for sale. And absolutely no need to creak your neck to look to the top of the buildings.

In fact, the only hint that we were in downtown Bear Creek was that it was just a little busier than the rest of the sleepy town. Instead of a cab rushing past us, a man with a brightly colored jersey swerved by on a mountain bike. His legs pumped the bike up the hilly, narrow street. Even though there were way fewer people than in a city, the sidewalks were super wide. A bell rang out as a preschooler and his mom opened the door to Bear Creek Creamery, an ice cream shop across the street from where we stood.

Thom paused, then crossed the road to peer into the shop window. "Yep," he said to himself.

"What?" I asked. It was the first time he had talked since we'd started walking.

"The ice cream lady. She isn't smiling. She never smiles."

Min raised up on tiptoes and peeked over Thom's shoulder. I squinted through the glass into the pink and mint green interior of the shop. Sure enough, the woman behind the counter looked like all the ice cream inside was sour. Her mouth was a straight white line and her shoulders scrunched. Her hair was tucked into a visor, except for a slash of straight bangs across her forehead.

"Why's she so upset?" I asked.

Thom sighed so long and heavy that it lay across my shoulders like a weighted blanket.

Min pointed to the marquee sign outside the shop, where the flavors of ice cream were listed: Jubilant Berry Compote, Merry Marmalade, Delightful Lavender, Marvelous Marshmallow, and Cheery Chocolate Cream. The sign said: *All ice cream created and made on site by Miss Juliet.* "How can you make ice cream like that and be sad?" she asked.

"Is *she* Miss Juliet?" I asked.

Thom nodded.

Inside the store, Miss Juliet put together a towering triple-decker cone. The mom laughed and grabbed extra napkins from the dispenser next to the cash register as the little boy danced in front of the counter. But the ice cream maker never cracked a smile.

My fingers itched to take out my notebook from my back pocket. *There's a story here,* I thought in my dad's voice. I just knew if he had been beside me, he'd be firing a text to a cub reporter, putting them on a profile piece about the sad ice cream maker whose flavors were full of joy.

Ding, ding. Min held open the door. "Let's go in," she said. She flashed a ten-dollar bill pulled from her back pocket.

Thom grinned and pumped his fist. He should smile more often. His whole face changed, in a good way.

Mom wouldn't like that I was eating ice cream before lunch, but she *did* tell me to go make friends. Wasn't eating ice cream together something friends did? I paused, watching Thom walk up to the counter. Min was standing holding the door open. Thinking of this whole mission—finding the newspaper and putting a reporter on the park story—as spending the day with *friends* made something squishy happen inside my chest.

Before this moment, the reporters at Dad's paper and my first-grade teacher were my only real friends.

Not that I didn't want friends. I liked the *idea* of them. But, in my experience, they were not all they were cracked up to be. Mom said it was because my brain worked differently—it was way more advanced and acted older than my emotions, which were standard eleven-year-old emotions.

I have something called a high IQ. Already Mom had been talking with Bear Creek Intermediate about its "gifted" program. I'm not so sure why they called it gifted; yeah, it was nice to be able to learn things quickly and figure out problems. But it'd also be a gift to be able to easily make friends, wouldn't it?

Not that all people with high IQs were like me; another girl in my old school's gifted class was the most popular person in the grade. This was just how my brain seemed to work: I barely had to think about things like reading and math, I spent lots of time figuring out problems (like how I was going to regain access to the park), and I overthought how to talk to people my own age. And by *overthought,* I mean I get stuck and end up blurting out maybe not-so-great stuff. Like that I had to leave because they were annoying me. People apparently don't like to be told that (even though Mom and Dad both told me friends shouldn't lie).

One girl in my old homeroom at Region 6 Charter told everyone (including me) that I was Bossy McBossalot. And Alejandro in my old apartment building said I didn't know how to have fun. Maybe a part of me thought both comments were subjective and wouldn't hold up to fact-checking, but another part of me said nonbossy, fun people don't fact-check their friends. And considering fact-checking was literally the job of the reporters at the paper and, in a lot of ways, my teachers, that meant I didn't really have friends.

Do I have friends? Are Thom and Min friends? I watched Thom look over his shoulder for me. Min was still holding open the door. For me. It was a lot easier to hang out with them when we had a mission than it was if I had to figure out how to be all friendly and nice. I sighed. Maybe I should just tell them I felt squishy and had to go home. But . . . Merry Marmalade.

My palms got sweaty. My palms always got sweaty when I didn't know what to say or how to act around people who were supposed to be "friends." If I was doing something—like working on a story—I could stay focused. I didn't spend too much time thinking about if I was smiling enough or too big. I didn't try to come up with what I should say next or tell myself to be quiet. I knew how to *be*.

Min raised an eyebrow. "You *coming*?"

I wished Dad were here. He always knew how to stop my palms from sweating before my squishy heart started pumping out bad ideas like *run home* or *correct their grammar* (it's *Are* you coming, Min).

I pushed my reporter's notebook farther into my back pocket, mostly just to make sure it was still there. Dad was the one who had first handed me a reporter's notebook. It was before Jenny Speilman's birthday party last year. I was in the backseat of Dad's station wagon, watching Alejandro whisper something to Jenny that I knew was about me. I had from the sidewalk in front of Dad's car to Jenny's doorstep—about twenty-two steps—to figure out how to be fun. I quickly came up with a plan: I'd push Alejandro to the ground, stand over him, and snarl, *"See, Alejandro! See me laughing! Who's having fun now, Alejandro? Me!"* Like I said, my squishy heart sometimes has not-so-great ideas.

Dad must've picked up on my feelings because he had turned around in the seat and stared at me in that dad way where you can't look away even (especially) when you'd really like that option. "I used to get nervous before going to parties."

I rolled my eyes at him. Dad? Nervous? Never. He was the bravest person I knew.

He nodded. "I'm serious, Nell. It wasn't until it became my *job* to talk to people, to ask them questions, that I kind of got over it. I realized that talking to friends wasn't all that different from scouting out a story for an article. People want to share their stories. If they see you're a good listener, see that you care about their stories, they'll like being around you."

"How do I show them I'm a good listener?" I mumbled.

He smiled and picked up a reporter notebook from the pile in the passenger seat. He flipped it to a clean page with one hand. "Here," he said. "Tuck this in your back pocket.

Pretend you're working for me." He turned around in his seat and stared ahead. "I'm going to need at least two profile pieces on people you've talked to at the party by the time I pick you up."

"So . . . just ask people questions?" I asked.

"That's all there is to it," Dad said. "Well, that and listening to their responses. Asking follow-ups. You know the drill, Cub."

I gulped but got out of the car and had tucked the notebook into my back pocket. It wasn't until I was at the doorstep that I realized he hadn't given me a pen. But that was okay because maybe Alejandro would've said something mean about people who took notes at a party. (You know who wouldn't be featured in my profile pieces? That's right. Alejandro.)

I even remembered what I had said to Jenny as I passed by her. "Happy birthday, Jenny!" Just like that. And she had smiled back at me.

You know the drill, Nellie, I told myself now as I stood outside the ice cream shop.

I could keep thinking of the mission—*find the newspaper; give them a tip to cover the park story; wait for the investigative journalist to uncover what's going on; return to the park. Alone.*

Friendless and lonely, go back to the swing to contemplate how life brought you to boring, dull Bear Creek.

To be honest, the mission didn't seem quite as important when my mind spat it out that way.

Maybe getting ice cream would be a way to scout out more information about a second story—one about Miss Juliet. *This is just story research,* I told myself as I stepped through the door. *I'm researching stories* and *I'm hanging out with my friends.*

CHAPTER SIX

WE STOOD IN FRONT of the creamery's counter, gazing at the giant tubs of swirly, delicious ice cream.

"What'll it be?" Miss Juliet asked. Her face was made of lots of straight edges. Straight line of bangs across her forehead. Straight cheeks hanging like messenger bags on either side of her face. Her eyebrows were straight dark brown slashes. Her mouth was a thinner, slightly pink line.

"Which one's your favorite?" Thom asked.

Miss Juliet flinched. But after a moment, she said, "I hear the Merry Marmalade is good." My mouth watered as I looked down at the tub she pointed to with her metal ice cream scooper. It was full of creamy vanilla with little streams of orange throughout.

"You *hear* it's good?" I repeated, my fingers itching again for my notebook.

"I've never tried it," Miss Juliet said with a sigh. Somehow the lines of her face got even deeper.

"The little spoons for samples are right there," Min pointed out. "Why don't you try some?"

Miss Juliet shook her head. "I lost my sweet tooth." She reached for the basket of tiny spoons and gathered some Merry Marmalade on one, which she handed to Thom.

His eyes closed as he tasted it. "Mmm," he said, and then slipped the spoon into a plastic baggie tucked in the pocket of his hoodie. Miss Juliet glanced at Min and me with a raised eyebrow. Both of us nodded, and she scooped up more onto two new sample spoons.

My eyebrows scrunched together as she handed me mine. It even smelled divine. "But don't you make the flavors? It says so on the sign."

Miss Juliet's chin popped up a little. "I make every ice cream sold in the creamery."

"I'll have two scoops," Thom said.

I popped the spoon into my mouth and gasped. It tasted like going to the carnival with Dad, when we would get orange popsicles, only somehow sweeter. "Same," I piped in.

Min nibbled her bottom lip, then asked for a sample of the Cheery Chocolate Cream. Then a sample of the Delightful Lavender. Then Jubilant Berry Compote. Miss Juliet gave her a sample of Marvelous Marshmallow before she could ask for it. She finally ordered a scoop of Lavender and one of Chocolate Cream. Maybe Min was smarter than I thought.

Soon we settled to eat our ice cream at one of the bistro tables in the shop. Miss Juliet closed tubs and wiped down the top of the counter after ringing up Min's payment.

"Are you lactose intolerant?" I blurted when Miss Juliet turned her back to clean off the scoopers.

"My mom has that!" Min said. "If she eats cheese, she has to go to the bathroom for an hour. It's disgusting. Then we have to open windows, though Dad says we shouldn't mention it because it makes Mom self-conscious. We had pizza two days ago, and I don't think I'll ever be the same after what I've experienced." She put down her spoonful of chocolate ice cream.

I shook my head at Min. To Miss Juliet, I said, "So, are you allergic to ice cream?"

Miss Juliet stilled but didn't turn around. "No," she said, her voice quiet. "That isn't it." She then went through a door to the back of the shop.

I quickly pulled my notebook out of my back pocket. I yanked out the pen I had jammed through the wire ring and flipped one-handed to a fresh page. Across the top, I wrote the word *WHO* in capital letters. Below it, I wrote, *Miss Juliet, owner and ice cream maker at Bear Creek Creamery.*

"What are you doing?" Min asked. I ignored her.

"Nellie? Nellie? Nell? Nellster? Nellieson? McNellieface?"

I sighed. She wouldn't stop; I knew that from the hour and a half that we had spent up in her treehouse when Mom and I first moved in and all I wanted was for her to know that I did not want to talk. But talking is Min's favorite thing. I muttered, "I'm taking notes."

"On what?" Thom asked.

"A potential story." I looked up for a second. "When we go to the newspaper to ask the crime reporter about whatever is going on at the park, maybe I could swing by the features desk and pitch them a profile piece about Miss Juliet." I kept my voice low so Miss Juliet wouldn't hear me.

Both Min and Thom tilted their heads as if I had started quacking like a duck instead of saying short, easily understood words. "I think there's a story here, so I'm taking notes. You know, scouting out **the big five**."

"The big five?" Thom echoed.

I nodded and turned back to my notebook. Thom scooted closer, and I felt Min hovering over me, reading what I wrote upside down.

"The first is *who*." I pointed to where I had written *WHO?* and Miss Juliet's name. "Now, I just need some descriptors."

I scribbled:

- Parent-aged
- Thin and tall
- Straight-line face
- Doesn't smile

"Add *seems sad*," Min whispered.

"That's implied by *doesn't smile*," I muttered, but I added it anyway.

"What are those little dots for?" Thom said.

"Dad calls those bullets. He says not to waste time writing whole sentences in a notebook. Just note observations in the moment or as soon as possible, because reporters who don't take careful notes make mistakes." My mind spat out Dad's real words in his voice. ("Trust your notes, not your memory,

Nellie. I don't know how many times I have to tell that to cub reporters before they believe me.")

Then I drew a slash across the page to make a division. I wrote *WHAT?* right under the slash and added: *Makes delicious ice cream that she never tastes. Names them for happiness/ joy but seems sad all of the time.*

Min nodded. "Underline *sad,*" she whispered. I ignored her.

Another slash on the page and then the next question. *WHERE? Bear Creek Creamery, the ice cream shop downtown.* And then I added more bullets with a description.

- `Small, cozy shop with pink tabletops and mint green stools`

- `Smells like sugar—maybe from the ice cream cones?`

- `Bright and clean`

Thom tapped his finger on the next line. "Add *seems like it should be happy.*"

After I did, I glanced around, taking in more detail, and then added:

- `Only picture on the wall is an old photo of a little girl and a woman, both of them holding bowls of ice cream.`

"Maybe the little girl is Miss Juliet!" Min said. But I thought the photo looked too old for that. Miss Juliet seemed about my mom's age, and I had seen Mom's childhood photos. They weren't black-and-white like the one on the wall. I added, *Miss Juliet?* and made the question mark extra big so I'd remember that I doubted it.

Another slash then, *WHEN?* I wasn't sure how to answer this one. It'd take time to research when Bear Creek Creamery began and when Miss Juliet started to make ice cream. It'd probably take even more research to figure out why she was so sad or who was in the picture. In both of those cases, I'd have to talk with her—ask her direct questions. I shoveled a melty bite of ice cream into my mouth. It dissolved almost right away, filling my mouth with so much deliciousness I didn't even mind leaving the *WHEN* unfinished. I just flipped to the next page for the final question.

The big one, as Dad used to call it. Across the top of the page, I wrote *WHY?*

Thom pulled in a big breath. "We're going to need a lot of ice cream, I think, before we can answer that one." Min giggled and clapped.

Maybe a part of me—a small part—didn't like that Min and Thom were kind of acting like they were going to pitch this profile piece along with me. But a bigger part of me—one that I thought Dad would be proud of if I told him about it later—was warm and happy that they wanted to work on it, too.

I swallowed. "Well, I guess I get paid my allowance tomorrow. I mean, that's when Mom is supposed to give me my allowance. If you guys want to meet here again . . ."

"*Yes!*" Min cheered. Thom smiled and nodded.

"But right now," I said, flipping shut the notebook with a satisfying clap, "we've got to get to the newspaper."

———————————

The newsroom of the *Bear Creek Gazette* was four blocks away from the creamery. As we walked, we passed old men sitting on lawn chairs outside of Bear Creek Hardware. Then we walked by a woman and her tiny black and white dog heading into Bear Creek Pet Supply. (Min made us follow them inside so we could whistle at the birds, and Thom added a sprig of catnip from the plants inside the store to his mysterious baggie.) Next, we went by Bear Creek Barber, where giant storefront windows showed stylists washing or snipping at people's hair. It even had an old red, white, and blue striped pole. Thom made us laugh by sharing that when he was in kindergarten, he told the class he wanted to grow up to be a barber pole. I told him about my cousin who had wanted to grow up to be bacon.

"Is everything in Bear Creek named after Bear Creek?" I asked. It was like the whole town was on a mission to remind me that I wasn't in the city anymore.

"Not everything." Min pointed across the street to a big red-brick building. The whole bottom floor seemed to be floor-to-ceiling windows, giving us a peek inside to a huge array of mismatched tables and chairs. Along the window was a painted-on sign: *Welcome to Wells Diner! Formerly Bear Creek Diner*. I sighed.

"The Wells are kind of new to Bear Creek," Thom said. "They moved here three years ago."

"Three years ago is new?" I asked as we turned the corner toward the newspaper office.

Thom shrugged. "Not much happens around here."

A man walking by us with a big cardboard box in his hands laughed, but in a way that sounded the opposite of happy. "You can say that again, kid." I noticed the box was filled with notebooks and newspaper clippings.

"Here we are," Min sing-songed. Everything she said came out like a sing-song.

In front of us was a squat, dark building with *Bear Creek Gazette* displayed on the front in the same type as the newspaper's **masthead** (that's the part that goes along the top of a newspaper). In front of the building were three newspaper stands and a flagpole with the American flag flying. A real newsroom was behind those doors.

"Let's go in!" I caught myself bouncing like Min and immediately stopped.

CHAPTER SEVEN

THE SMELL OF THE newsprint and chatter of reporters and editors rushed over me as I opened the door and walked into the building.

Know how houses have a certain smell? Thom's house smelled like pie and lavender. Min's house like lemons. Grandma's house like licorice and mint. I'm not sure what my new house smelled like—probably cardboard boxes because we still hadn't unpacked most of our stuff.

To me, newsrooms smelled like home. Old coffee, newsprint, stale pizza. Maybe that doesn't sound like a perfume someone would want to bottle up and spritz around, but I breathed it in so deeply that I went up on my tiptoes.

I glanced around, looking for the news desk. At the front of it would be my dad. Or rather, the person who had the same job that my dad used to have—news editor. That's the person who's in charge of staying on top of everything that's going on in the next day's newspaper. The news editor also puts the right reporters on the breaking news; whoever it was would know who I should talk to about the mischief at the park.

But this newsroom was different from my newsroom. First of all, it was much smaller. That was to be expected, I guessed. Around the newsroom signs hung from the drop ceiling. *News, Features, Editorial, Photo,* and *Sports.* Under each were a cluster of cubicles arranged in little pods.

A couple of things were the same. Attached to poles around the room were televisions, each tuned to a different channel. Police scanners buzzed from the pod under the *News* sign.

Just behind the newsroom was another room full of people in suits and ties. That had to be the advertising section, where salespeople sold ad space for the newspaper. Most people think newspapers are funded through subscriptions for delivery to people's homes, but Dad told me the ads were "a necessary evil" because advertising was actually "the bread and butter" of the paper. Mom had whispered that the advertising department probably thought the news stories were a "necessary evil" to their lists of ads.

"May I help you?" An elderly woman with puffy white hair and bright pink lipstick stood behind a counter at the entrance. Min and Thom both turned toward me. I straightened my spine. "Yes," I said. "I'm here to give a scoop to the news editor."

The woman's blue eyes rounded the way older people's do when a kid says something the way an adult would. Her mouth twitched. I hate mouth twitches like that. Next, she was probably going to say something like "oh, you're so *adorable*!" and maybe try to pinch my cheeks. I stiffened my face, making it as unpinchable as possible.

She must've gotten the message because she picked up the phone receiver and punched in a few digits. I heard a phone ringing in the distance. "Andy, you got time to take a tip from some neighborhood sources?"

Soon she ushered us through a little half door and we were officially in the newsroom. I looked around. The smell was just right, but what I saw and heard didn't measure up.

For one thing, the reporters were mostly young, like just a year or two out of college. No old reporters in wrinkled suits sitting with their ankles crossed on their desks, staring into space with a pencil in their mouths before suddenly bursting into motion, pulling the computer keyboard closer and hunching over it as they typed.

"Wait here," the older woman said. "Andy will be right with you." She strode back to the front desk, where a delivery person was tapping a little bell.

I looked around again, puzzling out what else was off about this newsroom. It was the boxes. Just like the grouchy man who passed us on the sidewalk, about a half dozen people were either holding boxes or filling them up with the stuff on their desks. At the cubicle closest to us, the phone on the desk rang. The woman filling up a box picked it up, paused before greeting the caller, and finally said, "This is the *Bear Creek Gazette.*" She listened for a few seconds and then said, "I'm sorry, sir. I can't help you with that. This is my last day. I'll transfer you to someone who can." Across the newsroom, a phone rang again and again, unanswered.

The noise was off, too. Yes, it had the police scanner and the televisions. But the *buzz* of a newsroom was missing. My dad's newsroom was filled with reporters volleying ideas, photographers dashing on the way to their next assignment, editors shouting across the room to each other. This newsroom sounded like Miss Juliet looked—too sad for its surroundings.

"Excuse me," I said to the woman who had just transferred the call. "What's going on?" I pointed to the box.

The woman sighed and pushed her hand through her bangs. When she smiled it didn't reach her eyes. "Layoffs. Andy just told most of the copy editors and reporters that we're out of a job, me included. I was the municipal beat."

My stomach clenched. That's what happened to Dad's newsroom, too. Not enough sales and subscriptions, so the paper started eliminating jobs one by one.

"I'm sorry," I mumbled. I didn't realize I was rubbing my chest with my knuckles until the reporter squeezed my arm.

The woman sighed, then dropped her hand to hoist the box onto her hip. "That's the way it goes in this industry."

As she walked away, Min nudged my side. "Copy editor?" she whispered.

"Someone who reads over **copy**—articles—and points out mistakes," I whispered back.

"You'd be great at that," she said.

Shows what you know, Min. I'm a reporter.

"She said something else. Municipal beat? What's that mean?" Thom asked. He leaned forward, sniffed a wrapped throat lozenge the reporter had left on her desk, and slipped it into the baggie in his pocket.

"A beat is a topic or area that a reporter covers. So, like, crime beat would be in charge of staying in touch with police, you know? And municipal beat is in charge of covering town meetings and stuff like that."

How was a newspaper going to do its job without a reporter covering the town news?

A man using a white cane headed our way. His tie was mostly undone. "Can I help you kids?" he asked once he was in front of us.

Min nudged me. I cleared my voice. "I'd like to speak with the news editor."

"That's me," the man said. His eyes drifted from me to Thom to Min. "I'm Andy Walters. Is this some kind of field trip? It's not a real good day for tours, I'm afraid."

I pulled the reporter notebook out of my back pocket and flipped it open to the page about the park. "It's about what's going on at Bear Creek Park," I said. "A man says he was attacked, and some pranks were pulled on drivers' cars parked in the lot. The police chief seems to think it's vandals. I'd like to know what the paper found out about it. Who's covering it?"

Andy rubbed at his eyes under his glasses. "This is about Hank, right?"

"Yes," I said. Min nudged me again, this time to give me a thumbs-up. I shook my head at her. *Be serious, Min!*

"We're not covering that story," Andy said.

"What? But I can't go to the park until it's figured out!"

Andy sighed. "Listen, it's a nonstory. Maybe if I had an extra reporter, I'd have someone hang around and scout something out, but if you haven't noticed, reporters are on short supply here."

"But how are people going to know if the park's safe?" I asked. "That's your job."

Andy sighed. "We just don't have the resources. Most of our stories are national now, picked up through the wire. I'm writing what I can, but we're not what we used to be."

Thom, who had been searching through his bag of smells, looked up. "What about the ice cream maker?"

"Miss Juliet?" Andy asked, his forehead wrinkling. "What about her?"

"She's sad," Thom finished.

I cringed. Suddenly it sounded like such a boring story idea.

Andy blinked. "Okay."

Min nudged me again. "Nellie says there's a story there. And she knows because her dad was a newspaper man."

Thom sidestepped away from me. Something flashed over Andy's face. "You're the Murrow kid, right? I heard about your dad, heard you and your mom were moving here."

"Yes." I straightened my spine. Dad's newspaper had won a big prize a couple years earlier for a profile on a teacher who became a breakout opera star in her fifties. I wasn't surprised he had heard of Dad.

"And how is—"

"Fine," I snapped. "He's in Asia." Thom took another side-step, but Min pressed against me. I elbowed her away.

"Oh," Andy said, his forehead wrinkled again.

"Anyway, I need to get to the park. And I can't until this story is out and everyone knows it's safe to go there. The newspaper can fix that. The newspaper is *supposed* to fix it."

The telephone rang. And then another phone at an empty cubicle started blaring, too. Andy sighed again. "Sorry," he said and turned around to head back to his desk.

"But what about the park?" I asked again. My heart squished up, thinking about not being allowed back on the swings. It was the only place I really could talk to Dad. I had to tell him how much this newsroom needed him.

Fact: A newsroom wasn't supposed to be sad and full of boxes and news editors who told sources to go away. *This isn't right!*

I must've said that last sentence aloud without even thinking, because Andy paused. He half turned back. "I know it isn't right, kid. Believe me."

"But someone has to write these stories. Bear Creek needs to know."

Andy shrugged. "I can't help you. Things are just different here now." The phone trilled again and Andy half turned away from us.

"But how are people supposed to find out about the park?"

Andy threw his hand not holding the cane up in the air. "Write it yourself!"

I stayed in place, watching him retreat, until I felt another nudge at my side. I was ready to yell at Min to leave me alone, but it was Thom.

"This isn't right," I whispered again.

"Maybe," Thom said. We stood there for a long while.

By the time I was ready to leave, Min was back at the counter waiting for us while she talked with the older lady. "So then my mom said it was raining, and I said it was barely sprinkling, and I totally beat Nellie down the slide even though she pretended she didn't care, and then the man said,

'I was attacked!' and then Nellie told him he wasn't before the police officer could even say that, no, he wasn't, and then the drivers of cars were like, 'Oh no! My wipers!' and now Nellie says there's a story there, but she says that a lot and I don't know what it means except we can't go back to the park and—"

"Well, not much you can do at the park," the old woman said, beginning to speak right over Min. "I've been saying for years that we need surveillance cameras there. Bound to get hoodlums sooner or later. Always happens."

Min continued as if the woman hadn't talked. "Mom says she's going to keep an eye on us, but I snuck out this morning and we used my allowance for ice cream, and that's another story—"

The old woman continued, too. "But if anything really had happened, I'd hear about it from Arlene Austin; she's always on that bench like it's her job or something. Meanwhile, here I am, eighty-two years old, still filing papers and answering phones at the newspaper, earning my keep while she just feeds those darned birds—"

"—I don't know how being sad is a story when I'm always happy and no one's ever said, 'Oh, there's a story with Min being so happy'—"

"—Gonna end up with bird flu. That's what's going to happen. I done told her, too. 'Arlene, you've got to talk to people once in a while. *People.* Not just spend days sitting there on a bench breathing in bird germs. Be useful. Come in here, why don't ya. Answer some phones. Like I do.' Even though I'm eighty-two years old. I still can be productive, you know."

"—I could write a story about being happy. Fill it up with hearts, and unicorns, and rainbows, and sparkles, and—"

I couldn't handle this. Friend or not, I could not handle discussions of unicorns and sparkles *in a newsroom*. I pushed by them and out onto the boring old sidewalks of Bear Creek.

CHAPTER EIGHT

THOM SAT BESIDE ME on the sidewalk while we waited for Min outside of the so-called newsroom. None of this was right. Nothing. There were supposed to be reporters there, ones who could get to the bottom of this story so I could get back to the park, sit on the swings, and feel normal, even if it was just for a little bit. And the journalists were supposed to have welcomed me into the newsroom, maybe thought it was cool that a kid was so interested in their work. Maybe let me hang out there, opening mail or something. Maybe give me a chair with wheels and my own space at the corner of someone's desk. A place for me.

This was supposed to be a place for me.

But there wasn't a single spot for me in Bear Creek.

I bowed my head, but Thom didn't seem to notice the wetness on my cheeks. He just sat there, leaning in a little so his body brushed mine, reminding me that he was there. I took a big, wobbly breath.

"I miss my granddad," Thom said when I finally stopped blubbering. I rubbed at my eyes. *His granddad? Why was he telling me this?* "He lived with us when he got sick. In the dining room. Ma turned it into a bedroom for him. For a long time after he . . . you know . . . I would sit in the corner of the room and take deep breaths." Thom put his hand inside his pocket where I knew he kept that baggie. "He smelled like mints. But the room doesn't. Not anymore. It is just a dining room again."

I pushed up to standing. "My dad smells like coffee."

The door behind us swung open and Min stepped through, still talking over her shoulder to the receptionist. "So, I'll drop off some stickers for you later, Miss Marcia, and you pass them on to the club, okay? Okay. Bye! Bye!"

"What was that about?" I said. Min's smile wobbled a little because my voice was sharper than maybe it should've been. She and Thom exchanged a long look with each other. I rubbed at my pathetic eyes and straightened up.

"Oh," Min said at last. "Miss Marcia, she has to do everything for her Scrabble club, even though she's the oldest member and the only one still working a full-time job at the paper—though they're going to make her take early retirement if things keep going the way they are. Not that it'd be *early* really since—"

"Yeah, I know—she's old!" This time I meant to snap. "What I mean is, what was the point of blabbering like that with her?"

But Min's smile only stretched. "Silly Nellie! Didn't you hear what Miss Marcia said?"

I growled. I didn't mean to, but that happens sometimes when words won't suffice for someone so aggravating.

Min's eyes widened. "Arlene Austin," she said in a small voice. "Miss Marcia told us who your source should be. Arlene Austin, the old lady who's always sitting on the bench in the park to feed the birds. She'd be able to tell you what really happened, I bet."

I gasped. "Min, you're a genius!"

"So, are we doing this?" Thom asked as Min bounced in front of us. "Are *we* writing the article since the paper won't?"

I got out my notebook from my back pocket and, just like Dad, flipped it one-handed to a blank page. "Oh, we're doing this!"

We quickly strode to the park. Min skipped, but I don't want to talk about that.

When we got there, Min stopped at the gate. "I told Mom I wouldn't play at the park," she said and crossed her arms.

"I told my mom the same." I leaned into her, pointing with my notebook. "And we're not *playing*. We're working."

Min dropped her arms. "That's lying."

"No, it's a technicality."

"Well, you're technicality a liar," Min said.

"That doesn't even make sense."

"You don't make sense," Min muttered, and sat on the curb glaring toward town while Thom and I went into the park. The bench where Arlene Austin was supposed to always be was empty, except for a couple peanut shells on the ground.

Chief Rodgers stood by the swings, arms crossed and glancing around. I started toward him until Thom grabbed my arm. "Isn't he going to tell us to leave?" he asked.

I held up the notebook. "Not today, Thom. Not. Today."

The sun must've been in Chief Rodgers's face or he was struck by a sudden headache, because as I got closer, he squinted and rubbed between his eyes. "Didn't Mrs. Kim-Franklin say you weren't coming back?"

"I'm here on official business." I waved the notebook and then yanked the pen from the wire ring. "I'm Nellie—"

"I know who you are, Nellie," Chief Rodgers said. "We talked two days ago."

"—Murrow, **freelance** journalist with the *Bear Creek Gazette,* and I have a few questions about incidents at the park."

"*Gazette*?" Chief said. "I knew times were tough there, but I didn't think they started hiring twelve-year-olds."

"She's eleven," Thom said, totally unnecessarily.

Chief sighed. "Go on."

"On the record now," I started. Thom nudged me, so I whispered, "That means we can write down what he says." Back to Chief, I finished, "What exactly has happened at the park and who is responsible?"

"Nellie, you were here. You know what happened," Chief said.

I held up the notebook again. "On the record."

He sighed loudly. "All right, so Hank says someone pushed him from behind as he left the restrooms. Knocked his hat off his head and disappeared before he could turn around and see who it was.

"Then that couple said someone stole a pair of sunglasses and the rubber from their wipers, and Rachel says her keys are missing."

"Says?" I echoed. "So, you don't think they're missing."

Chief Rodgers didn't answer.

"Suspects?" I asked.

"No description, no motive, no witnesses," he said. "So, no suspects. Unless you kids know of someone who can swat at a person and then disappear? Or if there's a black market for wiper blade rubber."

Both Thom and I shook our heads.

"Why are you here today? Working the case?" I asked.

"'Working the case'? There isn't a case, kid. Just a bunch of people claiming a bunch of different things. And then today, a jogger says she hears screaming. I get here, nothing but birds." As if they understood, a couple black birds took flight from the tree behind Chief Rodgers. "I get back to the station and, wouldn't you know it, another call. From this here park. Someone says their picnic lunch is demolished. Had it all spread out on the blanket, got up to throw the frisbee around, came back, and the sandwiches were gone, the drinks knocked over, and the basket toppled on its side. No witnesses, no suspects, no nothing!"

"You seem upset," Thom said. "You want to sniff my bag of smells?"

Chief Rodgers's mustache went perfectly still. His face flushed tomato red. He didn't move a muscle. Then, in a low voice, he said, "Did you just offer a police officer drugs, son?"

"No, sir," Thom said and pulled the baggie out of his pocket.

Chief Rodgers paused, then reached out for the bag. "And what is this?"

"A bag of smells," Thom said. And then he added, "You know, full of stuff that has a smell?"

Chief stared at Thom. "No, son. I do not want to try your bag of smells." He turned toward me.

"Now, worse of all, I've got a pint-sized reporter hounding me. Tell you what, here's an exclusive for you. A real scoop. Until we figure out who's messing with people at Bear Creek Park, the park is shut down."

"You can't do that!" My eyes snagged behind Chief Rodgers to the swings. "It's a public park!"

"And it's my job to protect the public. Until we figure out what's going on here, what's behind all this vandalism and mischief, park's closed."

"Well?" Min asked as we exited the park. "Did you find her?"

"Who?" I asked and kicked a rock. Maybe it wasn't the worst news in the world—the park closing. Maybe I could find a different place to talk with Dad. But the park was the only place that felt sort of like home in this whole strange town full of useless newspapers, sad ice cream makers, and maybe-sort-of friends.

"Arlene Austin," Min said. "The woman who's always at the park."

"She wasn't here," Thom said. "But the chief was." Quickly he filled Min in on what Chief Rodgers had said. Part of me was impressed with his memory because he hadn't been the one taking notes. But most of me was just sad.

"The park's closed?" Min said. "What are we supposed to do now?"

"Let's go home," I said and tried not to think about the piles of boxes that still hadn't been unpacked and the way I could sometimes hear Mom crying while she was up in her attic office.

"No," Min said. I looked up to see Thom and Min sharing an odd look. Then both turned toward me with arms crossed. "No, you're not going home to play with dolls and be sad."

"Those. Aren't. *Dolls*." My face felt like it was on fire.

"But you are *sad*." Min was leaning toward me with her hands curled into fists like a temper-tantrumming toddler. I straightened up and smoothed my hands on my shorts.

Thom kicked the rock back toward me. "Just because Chief Rodgers hasn't figured this out yet doesn't mean that we can't work on the story. Right?"

I glanced again at the swings and then at the notebook in my hand. Clearing my throat, I said, "If she's not here, where would Arlene Austin be?"

"With the rest of the old people in Bear Creek," Thom said.

And that's how we ended up at Wells Diner.

CHAPTER NINE

BY THE TIME WE backtracked to the diner, it was nearly lunchtime. Close enough, anyway, for most of the tables at Wells to be full of patrons. Thom, Min, and I stood by the door scanning for open seats.

Most of the diner was a big open room filled with dozens of wooden tables and chairs, each of them a different design and size. Mr. Wells must've gone to a bunch of tag sales and picked up the furniture for the restaurant. I mean, maybe he had (*Don't make assumptions, Nellie*). In the far corner, crocheted hats and blankets were displayed for sale; I recognized them as Thom's mom's work. The walls were decorated with dozens of framed photographs, some scenes of Bear Creek, with little tags indicating the price.

The back of the diner featured a long counter that ran the entire length of the wall and around the corner toward the door. The corner section behind the counter was the kitchen, open to the diner. There, a tall, skinny man threw pizza dough into the air, stretched it onto wooden paddles, topped it, then thrust it into the red-hot oven behind him. I didn't know if it was the heat or the hard work that turned his cheeks bright red. He wore a white T-shirt and mopped at the perspiration on his forehead with a cotton cloth.

On the other side of the counter corner, where there was a curved glass window like in a deli, a large man in a wheel-chair was building sandwiches and salads, his hands moving like blurs as he pulled paper orders down from a wire hanging over him and filled blue plates with meals. I saw a name tag with *Chef Wells* on it when he pushed his chair backward to grab a bag of potato chips.

At the edge closest to the door was a cash register. Stationed behind it was a girl about my age, maybe just a year or so older than me. *Gloria* read her name tag. She was writing an order on a slip of paper. She stretched up, put the slip of paper in a clip on the wire hanging above her, and shot it down the line to Mr. Wells. They had the same dark skin and smile with dimples; I guessed she was his daughter. As soon as the customer in front of her left, Gloria picked up the book on her lap and kept reading.

Beside her was a large whiteboard with the daily specials written in fancy cursive writing. Behind her, the entire wall was a blackboard with the menu written in bold, colorful letters, but there also was a basket of printed menus by the register.

I glanced again at the tables. Thom and Min were right; Wells Diner was the place to be for the old folks in town. The dining room was filled with older people playing cards, laughing with each other, or splitting a pizza.

I started toward them when Min grabbed my elbow. "We should order first," she said. She pulled a phone out of her back pocket and punched out a text. I was a little surprised that baby Min even had a phone, but I recovered quickly.

"I didn't bring any money," I said. *We're here to work, Min.*

But Min rolled her eyes and then skipped to the register while Thom and I trailed behind. "Can you put lunch on my mom's account?" Min asked.

"Dad?" Gloria shouted without looking up from her book. "That okay with you?"

"So long as her mom's okay with it," Mr. Wells said.

Min held her phone out to Gloria, who read a text from Mrs. Kim-Franklin okay'ing the lunches.

"What'll you guys have?" Gloria asked. Her long hair was pulled back into a high ponytail with curls spiraling out. Her big brown eyes passed over us, lingering on me a bit longer than on Min or Thom, which I figured was because I was new and Bear Creek didn't get new people often. I pressed my lips together while looking from the menu to the specials to Gloria, not sure how I would ever get the courage to talk to someone so cool. I suddenly felt the way Min must have felt whenever she was with me, like a baby next to someone super sophisticated.

Min ordered a slice of mushroom pizza and a soda, and then Thom asked for chicken noodle soup with extra crackers. I glanced at the menu and ordered the first thing I saw. "Um, I'll have a Pilgrim Shuffle."

Gloria smiled, her eyes crinkling at the edges. "For real?"

"Yeah," I said, smiling sophisticatedly back. "Sounds great."

Gloria grinned. "I came up with that one." She scribbled our order on a slip of paper and whipped it down the line.

"Told you, Dad!" she shouted. "Told you if we put it on the menu, someone would order it!"

That was when I began to question my lunch choice. Chef Wells sighed and began assembling our meals. I peeked closer at the menu for what the Pilgrim Shuffle actually involved. It was pumpernickel bread. *That was fine.* With turkey. *Also fine.* And mayonnaise. *All right.* Green leaf lettuce. *Good.* Cranberry sauce. *Huh.* Stuffing. *Wait.* Mashed peas. *No.* Cornbread. *Why?* Topped off with gravy. *What the—*

"Heck!" I shouted, then covered my mouth with my hands. Sometimes when I was thinking a bad word, my brain offered up a quick alternative. This one came so fast it blurted right out of my mouth.

"Excuse me?" Gloria asked.

I rushed down the counter to where Chef Wells was about to smear peas (*peas!*) on my sandwich. "Stop!" I shouted. He paused, the gloopy green gunk still on the spatula. "Could I have mine without the peas, please?"

The corner of his mouth twitched. "Sure," he said. "Any other alterations to the Shuffle?" Gloria strode down toward us. She looked at me with an eyebrow popped up. I pressed my lips together again and shook my head. "You sure?"

I nodded.

And then I saw the tub of steaming stuffing on the stove-top. "And no stuffing. Or cornbread."

Now Chef Wells was chuckling. "But lots of gravy, right?"

"No!" I shouted. Gloria crossed her arms, eyes narrowed in my direction.

"But, um, everything else," I said. Gloria sighed and went back to the register when a new customer dinged the little bell beside it. With a quick look in her direction, I lifted onto my tiptoes and whispered over the counter. "Just turkey and lettuce, okay?"

Chef Wells winked at me. "How about cranberry sauce on the side? I make it myself and it's powerfully good."

After our lunches, we looked around for Arlene Austin. Everyone we asked at the diner said they hadn't seen her yet that day. We'd need more information to track down our source.

Journalists aren't afraid to talk to people even if they're powerful, important, or really, really cool. Reporters are brave in their pursuit of their story. *The secret is to look confident, even if you aren't. Fake it until you make it, Nellie.* I took a deep breath, hearing my dad speak those words in my head, then held my notebook in front of me like a shield and went back up to the counter to talk with Gloria and Chef Wells.

"Excuse me," I said as I approached them. Gloria and Chef Wells were arguing and didn't hear me at first.

"I'm telling you, we need to mix it up a little," Gloria said. "People are sick of the same old, same old! Sales are down by ten percent this week."

Chef Wells countered, "Same old, same old is what pays the bills. Putting mushed-up peas on a sandwich? Drowning it in gravy?" He shook his head. "People want turkey! Just turkey!"

"Think about that special we ran last month. Where we put Mom's meatloaf recipe up there—the one with the cheese down the middle—everyone loved it!"

Chef Wells snorted. "That's because this is Bear Creek. It was a chance for folks to poke their nose and find out more about your mama."

Gloria's mouth puckered like her dad's words were covered in disgusting gravy. "They can get in line then, can't they?" she snapped.

Something twisted on Chef Wells's face. "I'm sure we'll hear from her so—"

"Whatever." Gloria huffed and then said, "We need to *do* something. Not everything can always just stay the same."

The words were heavy enough to make Chef Wells wince. I knew something about words like that. Mom would say stuff such as "We just need to put one foot in front of the other. Just keep moving forward"—seemingly about something simple, like emptying one of the boxes, but really, she was talking about something else, like moving away from what we used to have. I hated moments like that.

I even hated *seeing* moments like that.

Without realizing it, I started blurting, "If people are nosey—if that's what makes people buy new food—you could use *their* recipes. Like a contest or something. Say that you're asking local chefs to share their favorite meals and the best ones will be specials at the diner? You could maybe ask a reporter at the paper to cover it."

Chef Wells and Gloria turned toward me, Chef Wells with a giant smile on his face that was the exact opposite of Gloria's screwed-tight expression. But after a couple seconds, Gloria's face softened. She raised an eyebrow as she considered my idea.

"That's not bad," she said.

Has a face ever split in half from smiling? Because I thought that might've just happened to me. But then Chef Wells said, "You've got a mind for business, kid."

Smile gone. I did *not* have a mind for business. I had a mind for news.

News! I remembered why I had gone to the counter in the first place. "I'm working on an article for the *Bear Creek Gazette*. It's about alleged vandalism at the park."

Chef Wells frowned. "I've heard about that," he said. "All sorts of weird stuff happening there. One guy in here earlier this week swears someone threw a peach pit at him. Knocked him in the head. But when he turned around—"

"No one was there," I finished for him. "That matches what everyone else is saying. Stuff happens, but there aren't witnesses to anything."

Chef Wells nodded and turned toward his daughter. "Best to just stay away from the park, Gloria, until this business is sorted out."

"No!" I said, a little too loudly, I guessed, because both Gloria and her dad blinked at me. "We shouldn't abandon the park. We just need to find a witness, someone who might know if anyone new has been hanging in or messing around the park. A lot of people say Arlene Austin is almost always at the park."

Gloria nodded. "Yeah, she buys peanuts in the shell from us in bulk. Uses them to feed the birds. I have a bag waiting for her behind the counter." Gloria scanned the diner. "She's usually in on Mondays."

"Do you know where she lives? Or where she might be?"

Chef Wells pushed his wheelchair back a little as he, too, scanned the restaurant. "I'm not in the business of sharing customers' addresses," he said. "But next time she's in, I'll tell her you're looking for her."

I wrote my name and phone number on a blank page in my notebook, ripped it out, and handed it over to Chef Wells. He read what I had written. *Nellie Murrow, freelance journalist, The Bear Creek Gazette.* I braced myself for him to say something about a kid being a reporter. But he just went over to a corkboard behind the counter and put a thumbtack through the paper to keep it in place.

"Put in a good word at the paper for our recipe contest, Nellie. I think it's a great idea," he said as he turned around.

I was almost ready to skip away like that baby Min when I ran smack into a girl about my age. She had long red hair and huge, wide blue eyes. "Sorry," I said.

She nodded and moved to the side. As I started to walk away, she whispered, "Are you really a reporter?" I sighed but didn't turn back around. I expected this kind of doubt from adults, but not from other kids.

"Yes, I am."

The girl ducked behind the condiment stand and out of sight.

CHAPTER TEN

THE NEXT MORNING, I darted down the stairs and to the front porch to get our copy of the *Bear Creek Gazette*. All night I had lain in bed, staring up at the ceiling. Whoever had my bedroom last—maybe Gerald, Thom's old best friend—had put glow-in-the-dark stickers on the ceiling. They weren't bright anymore, just dim blobs. For some reason, they made me feel lonely.

I missed Dad. I tried to imagine what he would say about the article I was going to write. I knew if I could see him, his eyes would get crinkly at the corners when he heard I had spent the whole day with friends.

He'd tell me what to do next. I knew he would. But I couldn't talk to Dad in this house. I just couldn't seem to reach him here. The park was the only place where I could.

By the time the sun came up, I had convinced myself that the *Gazette*'s news editor had taken my advice and had looked into the park situation now that Chief Rodgers had closed it to the public. When more people heard about what was going on there, they'd pay attention and the vandals would be caught, and I would be back on those swings staring up toward the sky instead of at glowy sticker blobs.

I grabbed the paper from the stoop and sat at the kitchen table. Pushing aside the piles of letters, I smoothed it out. Quickly, I scanned the headlines. The whole front page was national and political news, except for one article along the right side about how school was beginning a week earlier this year because there were so many snow days last year. (Only six more weeks of summer break.) Dad would've shaken his head at the lack of local coverage. *What's the point of a local newspaper if folks can't get local news?*

Then I spotted the headline along the bottom: *Bear Creek Gazette closing doors.* I wanted to be surprised, but after seeing the newsroom, I had guessed this was about to happen.

After a 33-year stint as your community newspaper, the Gazette is closing its operations, effective in two weeks. That was just the kind of article Mom and Dad's old newspaper had to run a few months before we moved. Mom had kept that issue on the counter so long that one of the movers had used it to wrap up our water glasses.

I swallowed another sour feeling before flipping through the rest of the paper. Nothing about the park on page two, three, four, or five. And that was it. The rest were grocery store ads. I groaned and crumpled the paper in my fist.

"Hey there," Mom said from behind me. I had been so caught up in my search I hadn't heard her coming down the creaky steps. She cupped my shoulder in her hand. "What has you so worked up this morning?"

I glanced at her. She wore jeans and one of Dad's old T-shirts. Her hair was loose and hadn't been combed, let alone curled. Her eyes somehow looked bigger than they used to. Maybe because she was sleeping more at night and maybe because she hadn't been working on her book yet that day— they weren't tired. I thought about talking to her, unloading everything about the park and the mysterious vandals and the friends I sort of had now and about how the newspaper here was all wrong—how everything in Bear Creek (except *maybe* the friends) was all wrong.

But, like I said, this was the first time she hadn't looked tired or sad since we had gotten to Bear Creek. So, I just smoothed the paper back out again, folded it up, and handed it to her. "Nothing," I said. "I'm going to get ready."

"Ready for what?" Mom asked. She plodded over to the coffeepot and stared at it for a second. Coffee had always been this thing with Dad. Although we never had a lot of money, Mom said he acted like a millionaire about his coffee. We had this huge red and black coffee maker that also churned out espressos and lattes. It even had a section to grind the beans. Dad was always the one who took charge of it because Mom said a Mr. Coffee pot worked just as well for her.

"Dad showed me how to make Americanos," I told her. "I could show you."

Mom smiled. "That sounds nice."

Soon we were both sipping coffee at the table. My coffee, technically speaking, was mostly milk and sugar.

Mom smiled wide. "This makes me feel like myself again," she said. "Your dad, he used to make me a pot of coffee every morning, no matter how late he had worked."

"I can do that now," I offered.

"Let's have coffee together," Mom said. "Just like this. Me and you, planning our days. The way you and Dad used to go to the park and talk. We can—"

"I still talk to Dad at the park," I said. I got up and poured my coffee down the drain. It was too bitter. "Like I said, I need to get ready."

"Ready for what?" Mom repeated.

Ready for what?

A minute ago, I was getting ready to write an article for the *Bear Creek Gazette*. But now? That didn't seem big enough. Maybe I was ready for something else. Something bigger.

"Mom," I asked, "what would Dad do if his newspaper wouldn't—maybe couldn't—cover an important story?"

Mom paused, her hand stalling where it had been tracing the top of her mug. She cleared her throat. "You know your dad, Nellie. He'd find a way, even if he had to find a different newspaper that could cover the news."

I smiled. "That's what I thought. Can I borrow the printer for a couple hours?"

"Sure," Mom said. "I'm going to tackle some boxes this morning."

I darted over and gave her a quick hug.

"What's that for?" she laughed.

"Just 'cause." I looked around the cramped farmhouse and tried to imagine it without the boxes. Still pretty small. "I'll be right back." I ran upstairs, threw on some fresh clothes, and, without even pausing to make sure Min wasn't watching, ran across the street.

"Thom?" I called out, first toward the house, then toward the top of the tree, and finally toward the barn door.

"Nellie?" I heard him answer, but not from any of those three places. Instead, his voice drifted down from the top of the barn. There he was sprawled out on his back, staring straight up at the sky.

"What are you doing up there, Thom Hunter?" I yelled.

"Well, right now I'm just looking at the sky. But a minute ago, I was searching," he said.

"Searching for what?" What could he possibly be searching for up on top of a roof? *Was this one of those bag-of-smells meaning-of-life moments? Are friends supposed to know how to respond to this kind of thing?*

"Stuff," he said as he scooted to the edge. His legs dangled over the side of the roof. I heard some shuffling and then a little goat peeked over the edge, too. Thom put his hand on the goat's head. "This is Stuff."

"Oh!" I said, relieved we wouldn't be sharing our feelings after all.

Thom motioned for me to follow him to the back side of the barn where the roof sloped lower to the ground. The goat's enclosure was right against it. Thom stood with one foot on the fencepost and his bent knee on the side of the barn before wrapping his arms around Stuff and lowering the little brown-and-white goat toward me. I wasn't all that into hugging a goat first thing in the morning, but I guessed Stuff happens. It brayed in my ear as I put it on the ground. It smelled like that time Mom wanted to give composting a shot.

Thom hopped down after the goat.

"What's up?" he asked. Stuff rubbed its head into his side.

"How's the wi-fi in your barn?"

Thom didn't seem surprised by the question. Maybe friends are supposed to just roll with rando questions. "My parents work from home. Wi-fi could probably stretch to your house."

I bounced like Min. "Perfect!" I said and filled him in on my idea.

I put the pile of flyers in my backpack and called up the stairs that I was leaving. "I'll be back in a couple hours, Mom!"

"M'okay," she called back right away. I trotted up a few steps and saw her humming as she unpacked a box of books.

When I got to the porch, Thom was waiting for me. So was Min.

"We're making a club?" Min said. "I thought we were just writing an article? Now we're making a whole club! And the club's going to write a whole newspaper! All of us, together?"

I pulled a flyer out of my backpack and handed it to her.

Read all about it!

Newspaper Club

Bear Creek newspaper seeking local, focused reporters, editors, photographers, and designers. Will train!

Must be willing to work with a young news editor with a lifetime (11 years) of experience and collaborate with others, including Stuff. All ideas welcome, but Nellie Murrow is in charge.

Informational meeting 3 p.m. Saturday at the newsroom (Thom Hunter's barn).

"Why do you get to be in charge?" Min shook the flyer.

"Because it's my paper." I zipped up the bag and headed toward town.

"But *we* were writing the article together." Min pulled on my sleeve. "Besides, I thought we were writing it for the *Gazette*. To be printed in a *real* newspaper."

At this, I stopped. I turned toward Min and made my voice deep like Dad's when he was telling a reporter to do better. "My newspaper *will* be a real newspaper. Realer than that *Gazette,* okay?" I straightened my spine. "Besides," I said, "why would I give them our article when it could be in our own paper?"

Min blinked at me. Then a slow smile stretched across her face. "So, it's *ours*."

"What? Wait. It's—"

Thom stood shoulder to shoulder with Min. Both of them looked at me with the same smile.

"Yeah, fine," I said. "If you'd like to think of it as *ours,* I guess it could be considered *ours*." I took a deep breath. I was being really mature about all of this. I could almost picture Dad's eyes getting crinkly and Mom squeezing my shoulder like she had this morning. It felt *right* in a way that nothing had felt right since we moved to Bear Creek.

"But we each have to pull our weight," I added. "And that means putting up these flyers." I pulled a handful from my backpack and handed them to Thom, but when I turned to give a stack to Min, she was already skipping down the side-walk toward her home.

"Where are you going?" I shouted after her.

"Home! I need to design the thing at the top of my news-paper!"

"That thing at the top is called a masthead," I snapped. "It's the newspaper title. Ours is going to be *News by Nellie*. I already decided."

Min laughed. "Nah, I'll come up with something better."

I didn't realize I was huffing out of my nose until Thom nudged me with his elbow. "Stuff does that sometimes, right before he rams something. Are you going to ram something?"

"No," I grumped. I turned and pulled the backpack up my arm. The truth was, Min probably would come up with a great masthead. I shuddered remembering something and then whipped around. Cupping my hands on either side of my mouth, I shouted at her: "Not a single heart. You hear me, Min Kim-Franklin? There better not be a *single heart* on my masthead!"

"*Our* masthead," she shouted back and stuck out her tongue at me.

This whole newspaper thing might be the biggest mistake I've ever made in my eleven years in the business, I thought to myself. But then Thom tilted his head toward town and said, "Let's go," and I had another thought.

Maybe it was the best decision ever.

CHAPTER ELEVEN

READ ALL ABOUT IT!
NEWSPAPER CLUB

WHEN I ASKED CHEF Wells if I could hang one of the flyers in the diner, he came out from behind the counter and down a short ramp to the dining section of the restaurant to help us find the perfect spot.

"How about here?" he suggested, pointing to a blank square of wall behind the utensils and condiments. "Everyone in town will see it if it's here."

I thanked him and he went back behind the counter again. I stretched up on my tiptoes to hang the flyer. Too bad Thom had gone to the hardware store to hang one; he could've given me a boost. My arms barely reached the back wall and my stomach knocked over the ketchup when I tried.

"Hey, let me help you with that."

I turned to see a tall boy standing behind me. He had dark brown eyes that tilted upward when he smiled, light brown skin with freckles on his nose, and a camera hanging from a strap around his neck.

He put down a box of framed photographs and took the flyer from my hand. I moved to the side and he easily held it up against the wall. "This okay?" he asked.

"Yeah, that's great," I said.

The boy picked up the box and started to turn toward the front of the diner.

"Wait!" I called out. "Did you read it? The flyer, I mean."

He smiled again, and for some reason that made my face feel hot. I'd like to say that such a reaction is *not* a decision and therefore shouldn't be a big deal. Luckily, this boy didn't seem all that surprised by a girl blushing when he smiled. He scanned the flyer. "A newspaper club? That's cool."

"We need a photographer," I said and pointed to the box of prints he held.

"Oh, yeah? My work isn't really newspaper style," the boy said. He slid the box onto a table, took out a photo, and held it up. It was a landscape shot of the town bridge at sunset. It was beautiful.

I glanced around the diner, seeing all of the framed photos for sale. "Are all of these yours?"

The boy nodded. "Yeah, it's a fun hobby."

"Hobby?" I echoed. The photos could've hung in an art gallery. I held out my hand to shake his. "My name is Nellie Murrow. I'd like you to work at my newspaper." I sighed. "*Our* newspaper."

"Gordon Burke," the boy replied and turned back to pick up the box. "No offense, but I think I'm busy."

Just then Gloria came over to replenish the silverware in the bins. Gordon's eyes stayed on her as she read the flyer. "Hey!" she said. "This reminds me. I called the *Bear Creek Gazette* about the recipe contest idea and they turned me down. Said it wasn't 'newsworthy' enough for their last issues."

"We'll run it," I chirped, "in our newspaper. You could write it yourself, if you want. We're looking for an **editorial board**."

"Like an editor?" Gloria asked, her eyebrows rising.

"No," I quickly replied. "*I'm* the editor. An editorial board is the part of the paper in charge of writing opinion pieces on behalf of the newspaper. But you could also write personal opinion pieces, if you wanted."

"Is this, like, a school thing?" Gordon asked. "I have enough school stuff."

"No." I straightened my spine. "No teachers. No adults. Just us figuring out what we care about and focusing on that kind of news."

"Not school?" Gordon repeated. I nodded.

"Huh," Gloria said. "That sounds pretty cool."

"Yeah," Gordon echoed. He glanced again at the flyer. "So, you could write about stuff going on at the school and have it not be monitored by the school?"

I paused, making sure that he was talking about stuff as in events, not Stuff as in the goat. I was pretty sure he meant the first. "Yeah," I said. "We're an independent press."

Gloria crossed her arms and studied Gordon. "Would your mom let you do something like this?"

That's when I remembered where I had heard the last name Burke before—that morning in the article in the *Gazette* about school starting. The superintendent of Bear Creek School District was Dr. Valerie Burke. Gordon smiled, but only half of his mouth stretched back. "It'd really get under her skin."

Gloria laughed. "I guess you're in?"

Gordon shrugged but kept his smile. I wasn't so sure I liked him smiling like that at Gloria.

"The meeting is Saturday. At the newsroom," I said.

Gloria leaned toward the flyer again. "Which is . . . Thom Hunter's barn?"

"Yes," I said. "It has great wi-fi and Stuff."

The little bell at the counter rang out. "I'll think about it," Gloria said as she headed back to work.

"Yeah, me too," Gordon said, snapping a shot of the flyer before following behind her to talk with Chef Wells.

"Yes!" I fist-pumped to no one at all. But as I turned toward the door, I saw the quiet red-headed girl watching me from one of the diner seats.

Her gaze shifted to the flyer and then back to her lap. I pulled another copy from my backpack and slid it onto the table in front of her.

"You should join the Newspaper Club," I said.

The girl's face flushed as deep red as her hair and she didn't say anything as she picked up the paper. But when I started to walk away, she whispered, "I'm Charlotte."

I turned back to her. "I'm Nellie."

"I'm not . . ." Charlotte looked down at the flyer. "I'm not much of a writer. But I read a lot." The book beside her was thick with sticky notes.

"You're perfect for the club," I said. "See you Saturday."

I paused outside of Miss Juliet's ice cream shop. It felt strange to go inside by myself. For some reason, not having Min and Thom with me made me feel shy, especially when I saw Miss Juliet wiping her eyes with the bottom of her apron as I pushed open the door.

"Just a moment," she said.

I stood in front of the ice cream counter, looking at all of the merry flavors. *"Happy Jalapeño,"* I read out. "That sounds dangerous."

Miss Juliet laughed, even though her eyes were still glassy. "I tried to spice things up. The jalapeños are candied. Not too spicy at all. Plus, the dairy neutralizes the heat."

"I don't know," I said, shaking my head. "My dad would love it, though."

"Oh, yeah?" Miss Juliet said.

"Yeah, the hotter the better. Dad put hot sauce on everything, even mac and cheese."

"Well, tell him to—" Miss Juliet's eyes widened and then she looked at the floor.

"Puts," I said at the same time. "He *puts* it on everything. I'm not sure what kind of hot sauce they have in Asia, but I'm sure he still puts hot sauce on everything."

"I see," Miss Juliet said. Neither of us said anything for a moment, then her voice dipped low. "It's kind of funny, how everything—even taste—can change quick as a breath." She ran a sample spoon through Happy Jalapeño. "Would you like to try it?"

I cleared my throat. "Actually, I'm not here for ice cream today," I said. "I'm here on official business. Can I hang this flyer in the window?"

"A newspaper club?" Miss Juliet mused. She looked at the spoon, still filled with ice cream, and tossed it in the bin. "I suppose you could."

I pulled tape from the front pocket of my backpack and got to work posting the flyer in the window.

"You know," Miss Juliet said, her voice soft, "if you or your mom ever want to talk . . ."

"Great!" I chirped and threw open the door. "A features writer will be in touch for a profile soon."

———————————

That Saturday morning, I printed a sign-in sheet, slipped it into a clipboard, and placed it near the front of the barn on a hay bale. Stuff tried to eat it, so Thom moved him to the back of the barn.

After Min, Gloria, Gordon, and Charlotte arrived, we waited for a few more minutes in case anyone else showed up. I thought maybe Gordon would leave when Thom showed him his bag of smells, but Gordon just laughed. And Charlotte's eyes grew enormous when Stuff nibbled on her hair, but she stayed, too.

Soon the five of them were sitting on the barn floor, laughing and talking (everyone except Charlotte, who sat a little to the side but who was smiling). This looked nothing like a newspaper meeting. *Actually* . . . my brain thought the word in Dad's voice. And it was right; most staff meetings did start out this way, until the news editor brought things to order.

"Okay, let's talk about the first issue," I said in my grout voice, but everyone kept laughing and talking. "Lots to discuss!" I tried again. No one noticed.

Gloria glanced my way and cleared her throat. Gordon paused, and she tilted her head in my direction. Soon the rest of them stopped chatting and turned toward me, too.

I smoothed my hands on my shorts and started my speech. "Welcome, everyone, to the club. Bear Creek is in desperate need of an independent press. We're the ones to bring it to the town. I've got more than a decade's experience as a consultant for a major city newspaper. You're all bringing talents, too, which I'm sure we'll discover soon." A few staff members glanced at each other and Min's hand shot into the air. I pretended not to see it. "But I'll direct us as we release each issue of *Nellie's News*."

"That's not the name," Min cut in, hand still in the air.

I continued ignoring her. "Let's aim to publish monthly to start, with a weekly as a short-term goal and maybe even someday a daily issue."

Min stood up and pulled a giant piece of folded paper from her backpack. *"Our* newspaper—the one we're *all* making together—isn't *Nellie's News,"* she said. I looked at the paper she held up. It was a mockup of the newspaper.

"Wow!" Gordon said as Min passed the paper to him. "This is amazing!"

I sighed. He was right. Min had not only resisted the hearts, but she had designed an awesome masthead. Across the top was printed *The Cub Report* with a little round symbol of a bear cub. Under it was *All the news fit for printer ink in Bear Creek.* She even outlined boxes for different articles.

"So, what do you think?" she asked.

"The Cub Report?" I read aloud.

"Yeah," Min said. "Remember? You said new reporters are called cubs. I looked at other papers; the words underneath are kind of like the ones on a newspaper in New York."

"And the bear also is for Bear Creek. It's perfect!" Gloria added. Soon everyone was murmuring about the newspaper title.

"I suppose it works," I muttered. "It doesn't have the same ring as *Nellie's News,* but okay."

"Should we vote?" Min asked. She turned without waiting for my answer. "All in favor of *Nellie's News* raise your hand." Mine was the only one in the air. "*The Cub Report?*" Everyone else raised their hands. Even Stuff brayed. Min bounced and clapped like the baby she was.

"Fine," I said. "Okay, so now it's time to discuss positions. We need a photographer."

Gordon tipped his hand in the air. I wrote his name on a new piece of paper attached to the clipboard. I'm not sure why. It just seemed like the thing to do.

"Reporters," I said. "I think each of us could do that, but I'll be the investigative reporter."

"Unless I want to investigate," said Min. "Then I could be the investigative reporter."

"You're the designer," I said.

Gloria stood up. "I think we should figure out who's reporting on a case-by-case basis. That's my opinion."

I tried not to sigh. "Okay, that'll work. I'm the investigative reporter for the vandalism story at the park." Gloria, Gordon, and Charlotte all scrunched up their faces, so I quickly filled them in on what was going on at the park. Then everyone, even Min, agreed that I should take the lead on covering the story.

"I'll go by today and get some shots of the park," Gordon said.

"The park's closed," Min pointed out.

Gordon grinned. "I have a telescopic lens."

Thom cleared his throat. "I'll write about the ice cream lady." To Gordon, he added, "Can you take Miss Juliet's portrait?" Gordon nodded.

"What do you want to write about?" Gloria asked Charlotte, which was a good question, but which also should've been *my* question to ask. I let it slide.

Charlotte's voice surprised me by being deep. I expected a soft little whisper. "I'd like to be a copy editor," she said. "I've read about newspaper jobs and that's the one I think I'd like the most. I'd look for mistakes in the writing, like grammar issues."

"Perfect," I said. Did I know my staff or what? I totally had pegged her as a copy editor. "I'll be the news editor," I said superfast and then moved on before anyone could interrupt me. "And Gloria, you'll work on a story about the recipe contest."

"Can I do that?" Gloria asked. "I mean, since it's my family's diner? I thought newspapers were supposed to not take sides."

"Of course *The Cub Report* will be **objective**. That's super important. But maybe we can do something to make sure readers know that your piece is a column?"

Min crossed her arms at the same time as Gloria. "Why would she just get one column of a whole newspaper?"

"Not a column like that." I sighed. I didn't mean to; it just slipped out. "A column as in a **columnist**—a person who works at a newspaper who writes an opinion piece."

Gloria and Min both nodded. I asked Min if she could look into how other newspapers handle columnists in design and maybe do something similar.

Clearing my throat, I said, "Okay, it looks like our first issue will focus on three articles—alleged vandalism at the park, a profile piece on Miss Juliet, and the recipe contest. Gordon, maybe you could do a feature photo, too—something that could stand on its own in the newspaper?"

Gordon shrugged. "Sure, I guess."

"We'll keep the first issue to one page. Let's meet here tomorrow to check on our progress."

"Tomorrow?" Gloria repeated. "I'm going to need more time than that."

"Me too," Gordon and Thom echoed. Even Min said it, though she wasn't writing anything for the first issue.

A full day was a great deadline. Plenty of times at my dad's paper, reporters had to turn around copy (meaning unedited stories) in the span of an hour or two. But these guys were new, and maybe it would take more than a day for even me to figure out all of the sources at the park.

"Okay, how about four days?" I said. "We meet here Wednesday, same time?"

"What am I supposed to do until then?" Charlotte asked.

I rooted around in my bag until I pulled out a book: *The AP Stylebook*. I handed it to Charlotte. "Newspapers have a style—a way of writing stories."

"Is it similar to Chicago or MLA style?" Charlotte asked.

I was too overcome to answer immediately. When I did, the wrong words came out. "We're going to be good friends," I said instead of a reasonable response.

Charlotte's cheeks turned pink and she pushed the book into her backpack.

Min leaned forward and whispered, "But I'm her *best* friend. In the *world*."

"One more thing!" I called as the news staff began to trickle out of the barn. Stuff brayed behind me, but I ignored him. "You're going to need these." I pulled out three blank reporter's notebooks from my bag. They were heavy in my hands, even though they were small. I had found them in one of the boxes marked with Dad's name. I knew he wouldn't need them anymore, but it was hard to hand them out.

Gloria and Gordon took theirs with a smile and a thanks. Thom stared at his and sort of squeezed it with both hands. He didn't smile but nodded, and I remembered what he had said about missing his grandpa. "Thanks," I whispered to him, even though I was the one giving him something.

I watched them leave and for a moment my eyes flooded.

I sat down in the hay. Sure, there were many things to figure out—delivery systems, whether anyone on staff could actually write, taking on total cubs and teaching them newspaper style. But we were officially a club. I had the sign-in sheet to prove it. I took out my phone, again thumbing to Dad's contact number.

Behind me, Stuff grunted. Then I remembered that Min was still in the barn, too. I whipped around and there they were, standing side by side staring at me. "Is that him?" Min asked. She peered over my shoulder to the little picture of Dad on my phone.

I nodded.

"We both look like our dads."

I turned back to the picture. Yesterday Min and her dad had played catch in the backyard for hours. Mr. Kim-Franklin wasn't like his polished, ruffly wife; he was quiet and wore all black and gray like me. But when he played ball with Min, he glowed the way she does. He even bounced a little before throwing the ball to her. I guessed playing catch was their thing, sort of the way the swings had been Dad and my thing. (Maybe it sounds like I had been spying again; I hadn't. It's just my bedroom window was open and I could hear them laughing together for a long time.)

After a few minutes of Min just sitting next to me, I said, "You did a really good job on the masthead."

"I know," Min said.

"You didn't have to," I said. My heart squished up. "I mean, I know your mom is making you be my friend."

Min pushed my shoulder. "*I* decide who my friends are."

"But why?" I whispered. "I don't normally . . . sometimes people . . ."

"Even though you're bossy and hide your best toys, you have good ideas and are really brave."

"Oh," I whispered. "So, you *want* to be my friend?"

"For someone who is supposed to be so smart you can be really not smart sometimes," Min said. "And I'm not your friend. I'm your very best friend in the whole world."

"Oh," I said again. "Right. So . . . do you want to reenact stuff with my realistic figurines sometime?"

"You mean play with dolls?" Min asked and danced in a circle. But then she gasped. "Wait! What are you still doing here? Don't you have a cover story to write?"

CHAPTER TWELVE

AFTER THE MEETING, I swung by home to get an extra pen. Dad told me once about a reporter who had been sent out to cover the aftermath of a tornado. All sorts of experts were there from the weather service as well as people affected by the storm. She had the chance to get dozens of interviews and quotes but came back without anything decent all because her pen's ink ran out a half hour into the day and then her phone battery died, too. Since then, Dad always reminded reporters to bring two pens to every scene or interview.

I noticed a lot of the reporters used a blue and a red pen. The blue was to take down notes and quotes at the scene. The red was for when they were on their way back, to jot down their own thoughts about what they had seen.

But all I could find were black pens in the kitchen junk drawer. Most of the other pens were probably in Mom's office. I crept up the stairs, avoiding the super-creaky ones. The attic door was mostly closed, but I could peek in the narrow opening. Mom was at her desk, her laptop pushed back. She rocked in her chair. I could see the side of her face, enough to notice her smile. But I would've known that she was happy even if I hadn't been able to see her simply by the sound of her voice. That's how I knew she was talking to Dad, too. Only he could make her voice go soft like that. "You'd be so proud of her, Mike. She's venturing out every day, making friends. Everyone's been so kind. The people here, they're looking out for us like we're family, even though we just got here." She paused, I guess listening to Dad.

"The diner owner in town, he called yesterday to let me know Nellie hung up a flyer in the store. Something about starting a newspaper. I mean, of course she is. She's our kid."

I pressed into the door, my ear against it, but careful not to open it further. "I know, and you're right. I need to be doing the same—getting out there and making friends. And I will.

I'm just so . . . I'll get there, Mike. Nellie and I, we're going to be okay here in Bear Creek."

I swallowed down a sudden ache in my throat.

Mom had reception in her attic.

———————————

I went straight to the park after that, hoping that maybe it'd be open again. But the yellow tape draped across the gates clued me in that it was still closed.

Chief Rodgers wasn't there, but I found a sign reading that due to unusual circumstances, the park was closed until further notice. I jumped when a crow cawed.

"Kind of creepy, huh?"

I turned to see Gordon dropping from a tree beside the gate.

"Yes," I said. "Do they teach all of you how to climb trees like that in school here or something? It's quite strange."

Gordon looked up from thumbing through the images on his camera. "Huh?"

"Oh!" I said. "You mean the park. Yeah, that's creepy, too."

Gordon handed me the camera. It still hung from the strap around his neck, but I could see the small square image he had captured. A cluster of crows perched atop the swing set. Gordon thumbed through other images. Another showed the bare jogging trails. The third showed a dozen black birds bouncing around one of the park benches, beaks open as if talking with each other.

I stared at the images, not saying anything.

Gordon leaned back, but I grabbed the camera with two hands, staring at the park bench.

"Uh," Gordon said, "I could try again. I mean, if none of these will work . . ."

"Zoom in!" I ordered. "Here." I pointed to a corner of the tiny image. I glanced up at Gordon. His forehead was scrunched, but he pushed a couple buttons with his thumbs and soon the image zeroed in where I had pointed.

"There!" I said. "Do you see it?"

"What *is* that?" Gordon asked, squinting at the black strand of rubber hanging from the crow's mouth.

"Evidence." I bounced like Min. "Can you email or text this picture to me?"

Gordon rubbed the back of his neck. "Yeah, I guess."

"Awesome!" I cheered, scribbling into my notebook as I practically skipped toward town. "Great job, Gordon."

"Where are you going, Nellie?" Gordon called.

"To find a bird expert." I paused. I had no idea where to find a bird expert. I hated not knowing where to go next. "Do you know any?"

Gordon shrugged. "Mom teaches at the university sometimes. I bet there's an expert there. She's going later today if you want a lift. It's about a half-hour drive from here. I was going to go, too." He held up the camera. "I sit in on some photography classes sometimes." Gordon lowered his voice. "But don't tell my mom, okay? She thinks I'm there to skateboard."

———————

An hour later, Dr. Burke picked me up on the way to the university. I researched birds on my phone while she drove. Bird experts were called ornithologists. The college had a whole animal studies department, including a wing for ornithology. I chuckled a little when I read that on the website. *Wing*.

Dr. Burke gave me directions to the animal studies department and brought up a campus map on my phone. "Are you sure you're okay navigating on your own?" she asked, her mouth downturned. "Gordon, why don't you go with your friend?"

Gordon was circling us on his skateboard. Every time he wheeled by, Dr. Burke's frown deepened a little.

"That's okay," I said. "I mean, Gordon, you can come if you want, but I'm used to running around college campuses. I used to interview professors for fun while my mom taught journalism as an adjunct."

Dr. Burke's eyes widened. "Really?" She turned toward Gordon, her mouth hardening as he made the skateboard go in a small circle. "Just think, Gordon, how you could be spending your time more usefully following some passion."

Now I was the one with the frown. *Why didn't Gordon tell her that he really came here for photography classes?* But Gordon ignored the barb. "Yeah, I'll come along," he said. "Some cool ramps there." When Dr. Burke turned away, he held up his backpack, which was unzipped, showing me the camera tucked inside.

Dr. Burke sighed and then went to her class. Gordon slipped the camera around his neck.

We quickly found the ornithology department, which was actually just a large office with cubicles. The walls were covered in migration charts and every surface had bird skeletons or models placed on it. "Excuse me?" I called out as Gordon and I closed the door to the department.

"No late assignments accepted!" came a voice from behind a cubicle partition.

"I'm from . . ." I cleared my grout voice. *"The Cub Report.* It's a real newspaper. I'd like to interview an ornithologist, please."

"A real newspaper, huh?" A woman whose long, gray hair was tied at the base of her neck stepped out from behind the cubicle wall. She crossed her arms when she saw Gordon and me. "I don't trust journalists from reputable newspapers, let alone kiddy reports."

"The Cub Report is *not* a kiddy report," I snapped.

The professor held out a long, slim hand. "I'd like to see a copy, then."

My face flushed. "We're working on our first issue," I muttered.

The professor rolled her eyes. "Do you have an appointment?"

"No," I said, "but I just want to ask a few quick questions."

"No appointment, no questions," she said. "As the only research ornithologist in this university, my time is limited."

"It's about birds in Bear Creek!" I blurted, even though a journalist should always be collected. "I think they're upset."

The ornithologist professor sighed. "I don't have time for this." She walked back to her cubicle. "Animals are not people. They don't get *upset*. Professors, however, do, especially when their precious time is squandered. Goodbye."

"But—" I started. The professor didn't glance back.

"That was so rude," Gordon whispered.

"It's typical," I said after a moment, straightening up. "You won't be so surprised after a few issues. People think it's okay to be rude to journalists even though we're just doing our job."

We were back in the hall when the door to the office opened. I whipped around, hope making me smile like Min. But it wasn't the professor. A young Asian man stood in front of us, floppy hair swooping to the side across his head. He wore a T-shirt with the name of the university on it and a badge around his neck. I noticed a small bird sticker on the badge.

"Hey," he said. "I'm sorry about the professor. She gets stressed during migration season." He held out his hand to shake. As I shook it, he said, "I'm Patrick Tran, and I handle some of the ornithology research projects here."

I pulled the notebook out of my back pocket. "Can you go on the record, Mr. Tran?"

He shrugged. "I guess so."

Quickly, I told him about what had happened at the park. As I spoke, his mouth twitched. "Classic," he said.

"Classic?" I repeated. That was a reporter trick Mom had taught me. Instead of full questions, the best way to get a source to divulge more was with a little nudge.

Mr. Tran crossed his arms. "Do you have a murder in the park?"

"Yes!" I said as Gordon gasped, "No!"

Mr. Tran laughed. "Just checking to see how detailed your research was," he said to me. "Do you want to tell him or should I?"

I grinned. "A murder is what you call a group of crows. You know, instead of a flock."

"*Oh,*" Gordon said, stretching out the word. "Then there definitely was a murder at the park." He pulled up the picture of the crow with the long strip of rubber in its mouth and handed the camera to Mr. Tran, who thumbed through the photos, his smile stretching even more as he went through the frames.

"More and more research shows the ability of birds— particularly crows and ravens—to reason and feel. In fact, many researchers believe crows have the intelligence of a seven-year-old child. So as smart as you, really," Mr. Tran said.

I glared at him. "I sincerely doubt that." Brushing my hair off my forehead, I added, "Besides, I'm eleven."

"Right," Mr. Tran said, and he wiped his hand over his mouth like he was smearing away his smile. "I got into this field because of crows. My family rescued a young one that had been hit by a car. We nursed it back to health. It remembered us for years, swooping down whenever we were outside. The coolest part was that it taught its children to do the same."

Mr. Tran glanced behind him at the closed door. "Lots of researchers caution that we shouldn't romanticize subjects. It's tempting to people to try and think of animals in human terms, but that can be dangerous for their health."

"How would that be dangerous?" Gordon asked.

Mr. Tran shrugged. "Well, it's sort of the flip side of demonizing certain animals. Look at the big, bad wolf and how that played a role in the real animal's depopulation across the world," he said. "When we start morphing animals into human terms, we risk losing objectivity."

Objectivity was vital to journalism. As soon as a reporter became personally invested in a story she was working on, being truthful and fair in coverage was at risk. It'd be like reporting on a politician's actions despite already announcing that the politician was a bad person. That would cause bias, or favoritism, which doesn't belong in the news.

Mr. Tran continued, "There's a history of crows seemingly doing things like what's going on in your park. I'm not saying you have a crow issue, but I can tell you that crows have been known to head-dive people to get their attention, especially if they're too close to where the birds are roosting." He held up one finger. Raising a second, he added, "And they've been recorded stealing things, such as key rings." He unfolded a third finger. "And the windshield wiper is another on-the-record item crows have been known to take apart."

"Why?" I asked while busily scribbling down Mr. Tran's response. He paused while I whipped to a fresh page.

"Well, sometimes it seems they do it just because it's fun." He grinned. "They seem to like to play; messing with humans must be a fun game for them. But with all of these things happening at once, I'd think there might be more to it."

"Like what?"

The doorknob behind us began to turn. Mr. Tran's eyes widened and he ushered us down the hall. In a lowered voice, he said, "I'd start looking into what might've changed in the park."

Gordon and I went to the college library after interviewing Mr. Tran. I quickly brought up research on crows on one of the desktop computers. Crows lived in families, sometimes generations roosting in the same tree. Mr. Tran was right about them being as intelligent as a child—I watched videos of wild crows figuring out multiple-step puzzles to get a piece of food. I also read sections of research by ornithologists about how playful crows could be, but also how angry, particularly if someone blocked them from getting food.

"Look at this," Gordon said softly. He was sitting next to me, doing his own crow research. I leaned over to see what he had brought up.

It was a research project investigating why crows reacted the way they did when another crow died. Other crows gathered around the body of the dead crow. They cried out loudly and called to other crows to join them. "It's like they grieve," Gordon said.

I shook my head. "You're doing that thing Mr. Tran told us not to do. It says here they might just be trying to learn what killed the bird so they don't do the same thing."

Gordon didn't say anything for a long moment, just breathed in and out. For some reason, I couldn't look at him. Finally, he whispered, "Or they're recognizing someone is gone and letting themselves feel sad. I think that's probably pretty important, too."

I turned back to my computer.

CHAPTER THIRTEEN

WE GOT BACK FROM the university at three o'clock. I texted Mom, asking if it was okay if I grabbed something to eat at the diner and worked on my article. Something was nagging me, a feeling like I was missing some crucial piece to my story. I thought maybe if I sat in the diner with my notes, it'd be kind of like sitting amid the bustle of the newsroom. Maybe it'd help me figure out what I was missing. Plus, other Cubs— Gordon and Gloria—were going to be there, too. They could maybe help me figure it out. *Look at you, leaning on your friends,* I heard in Dad's voice. My eyes got crinkly at the thought.

Quickly, Mom typed back yes. Too quickly. It must not have been a good day.

"How'd it go?" Gloria asked after I ordered a slice of pizza. Gordon was talking with Chef Wells about some of the framed photographs he had up for sale around the diner; someone had bought a bunch of them all at once.

I shrugged. "I'm missing a few details." Mr. Tran had seemed pretty convinced that crows could be responsible for the vandalism at the park. But if I wrote that in my article without any proof, *The Cub Report* would be a joke. No one would believe it, even with the photo of the wiper blade rubber in a crow's mouth.

Chief Rodgers, sitting in the back corner of the diner, was dipping a grilled cheese sandwich into a bowl of Chef Wells's tomato chowder. I'd wait until he was done before asking him a few more questions. Mom had said it was rude to ask sources for information when they were out to lunch.

Mr. Tran had suggested we look into what could've changed at the park. But I had been going to the park every day since we moved here and, just like everywhere else in Bear Creek, nothing had changed.

At least, I didn't think so. Gloria was saying something else, but I tuned into what was going on behind me. Someone in running clothes passed Chief Rodgers's table. "Hey, Chief, when are the park trails going to be open again?"

"When I get some leads," said the chief, not looking up from his soup.

"Nothing?" the runner asked.

"It's an open investigation. Not discussing the details."

"Sure." The runner shook his head as he walked away. "You look real hard at work there, Rodgers."

"I'm having lunch. People can have lunch and still be working!"

Although Mom said interrupting sources was rude, *Dad* had always said that reporters should seize any opportunity to confront them. And Chief Rodgers *had* said it was a working lunch.

I nodded to myself.

"Ha!" Gloria called over her shoulder to her dad. "Second order of the special today. Pizza with peaches and arugula coming up!"

"What? Peaches? On pizza? No!" I yelped.

"You don't have to be rude about it," Gloria said. "I asked if you wanted to try it and you nodded."

"I was nodding at my own thoughts," I said. "I'd never nod for peach pizza."

Gloria's eyes narrowed.

"Don't worry," I said. "Once that column on recipes runs, people won't accidentally order specials; they'll do it on purpose."

Gloria's arms crossed. A few feet down the counter, Chef Wells chuckled.

"Boring old pepperoni it is." Gloria rolled her eyes.

I went over to Chief Rodgers, who was reading the *Bear Creek Gazette*. He sighed and pushed it aside. "Hello, Nellie," he said. "The *Gazette*'s closing, so I assume you're not here in your official capacity as a so-called reporter."

I pulled my notebook out of my back pocket, and he groaned. "I no longer freelance for the *Gazette*. I work for a different newspaper now."

"Sure, sure," said the chief, dipping his sandwich into his soup.

"Has anything happened to disturb the murder?"

"The what?"

"The murder," I repeated. "That's what a collection of crows is called."

He sighed and dropped his sandwich onto his plate.

"I thought you were working on an article about the vandalism at the park?" he said. "Now you're asking about crows?"

"Yes," I said. "Has anything upset them lately?"

"Upset them?" Chief Rodgers threw up his hands. "What exactly do you think police do, kid? It's not all sniffing bags of smells and checking in on birds' feelings, I can tell you that."

Gloria brought over my slice of pizza, muttering *boring* under her breath as she walked away.

"Just a few more questions." He groaned. *Reporters must be persistent,* I heard in Dad's voice.

Before I could ask another question, a plate rattled to the floor beside us. "What was that?" a diner squealed.

Chief and I both were on our feet, turning toward the action. A slice of pizza lay upside down on the diner's black-and-white tile floor. Hank, the middle-aged man who said he had been attacked at the park, rubbed at his tongue with a napkin.

"That was the special," Gloria said. "You ordered it."

"I said I wanted something special. Not something disgusting! Were those *peaches*? On *pizza*?"

Chef Wells rounded the corner. "I'll get a slice of regular. On the house, Hank."

"There's nothing wrong with that pizza," Gloria said. "Have a taste for adventure, people!" But she brought a mop and bucket out from a pantry and headed toward the flipped-over slice.

"Bit of an extreme reaction," I murmured to Chief.

"Ah, you know how it is," Chief Rodgers said with a shrug. He pointed to his tomato soup. "You like what you like. I count on Wells back there making this chowder every Monday at lunch. Just like we get tacos on Tuesdays. If he went and threw peaches in there, I'd be pretty sour about it, too." He dipped a piece of crust into the bowl. "We're all creatures of habit, I guess."

"Creatures of habit," I repeated under my breath. "That's it!" Suddenly, what had been nagging at me unsnagged. I jumped to my feet, accidentally upsetting my own plate of pizza.

"Really?" Gloria snapped. "I'm not cleaning that up, Nellie."

"Sorry!" I said and plucked the piece off the tile. I tossed it back onto the table, ignoring Chief Rodgers's grimace. "Birds! Creatures! Habit! *Peanuts!* That's it!"

"Yeah, yeah," Chief said and rolled his eyes. "It all makes sense now."

"The birds!" Sometimes when I got excited my thoughts rushed out like a faucet turned to full blast. Dad used to hold my face in his hands and tell me to breathe when I got like that.

I pressed my own hands against my cheeks, forcing myself to pause. But I was too excited to sit down again.

"There was a person—Mrs. Austin—who fed them every day. The receptionist at the *Gazette* said Mrs. Austin is always in the park. But she hasn't been lately. Not that day with Hank! Not that day when you put up tape and closed the park! Not in at least a week!"

Gordon, who had been hanging more framed photographs for sale around the diner, piped in. "Yeah, and she wasn't there the day I got those shots of the birds, either."

Chief Rodgers stood up and brushed crumbs from his lap. "Shots? You were shooting birds, son? At the public park?"

"Well, sure," Gordon said. He glanced at me and Gloria in confusion, before lifting his camera and going through the images to those of the birds.

"Oh," Chief said and sat down. "Camera shots."

"Yeah, of course," Gordon said and handed over the camera.

"Huh," Chief Rodgers said. I peeked over his shoulder; he had gotten to the images of the crow with the wiper blade rubber in its mouth.

"See!" I said, excitement taking over again. "Crows! They do this! They're super smart, and they do this kind of thing.

Something's wrong and it's not what's at the park—it's what *isn't*. Mrs. Austin! She fed them every day; they're acting out because they're hungry."

"Or because they miss her," Gordon said.

Gloria turned and called out to her dad. "Hey, Pops. When was Mrs. Austin in here last?"

Chef Wells rubbed the back of his neck. "Been at least a week. Maybe two." He pulled a landline phone from its holster on the wall and punched in some numbers. After a long pause, he looked back toward us. "No answer at Arlene's."

Chief Rodgers popped up again from his seat. He pulled the walkie-talkie strapped to his shoulder closer to his mouth and said something in police code.

"Let's go!" I said and tucked the notebook back in my back pocket.

Chief Rodgers pointed his finger at my face. "No. I'll debrief all the press after we check on Mrs. Austin."

Part of me thought of fighting—journalists are able to go to crime scenes, so long as they don't interfere. But a bigger part knew to hang back; I didn't know if I *wanted* to be among the first on the scene to discover whatever was keeping Mrs. Austin from the park. And a third part gave me happy shivers. Chief Rodgers had called me *the press*.

That night, someone knocked on our front door. *Min,* I assumed.

But when Mom opened it, she gasped so loudly I dropped my notebook and ran. It was Chief Rodgers and Gloria.

"I'm sorry to frighten you, Mrs. Murrow," the chief said.

Mom shook her head. "I'm being silly. Not used to seeing an officer on my doorstep."

Chief tilted his head in my direction. "Mrs. Austin is doing fine. She had the flu and was weak. She says she didn't want to bother anyone, but she was in rough shape. She's doing better now, and her doc says she'll be back to herself in a few days."

Gloria said, "I just dropped off some meals from the diner. You saved her, Nellie. If you hadn't put those pieces together about the crows, who knows how long—"

"I was just doing my job," I said. "Hold on a sec."

Mom's head swiveled among the three of us. Her eyes widened again when I came back holding my notebook. "On the record now," I said. "When will the park reopen?"

"That's the thing," Chief Rodgers said.

Gloria stepped forward, swinging a little basket in her hand. "We need to test your theory."

The next day, we met early at the park. Mrs. Austin sat on her bench next to Chief Rodgers. Min, Thom, Gloria, and I spread peanuts and bits of fruit in front of the bench.

At first the crows ignored us. Then a few squawked. Finally, a dozen or so swooped down. They hopped as they picked at the peanuts and pieces of diced-up apple. A couple flew up to perch on the bench behind Mrs. Austin. "I missed you, too," she told them.

Gordon crouched on the grass and aimed the camera in Mrs. Austin's direction as a crow hopped onto her shoulder. She laughed. "I didn't think anyone cared about little ol' me."

"Look around you, Arlene," Chief Rodgers said. "The whole town, down to its birds, cares."

Gloria nudged me. That's when I saw Charlotte standing half hidden behind a tree at the edge of the park, watching us. I waved to her, but she ducked behind the trunk. "What do you think is going on with her?" Gloria asked.

Kind of odd, wasn't it, that I always felt so left out because it seemed like everyone else made friends so easily. But now that I was in Bear Creek, where I had a whole club of friends, I was realizing that lots of people struggled to make friends. Even Mrs. Austin thought no one noticed her, when really a whole murder of crows thought of her as their friend. (If, you know, you bought the whole animals-have-feelings idea.)

I glanced again at Mrs. Austin and saw a crow land at her feet. It let out a soft call that sounded a lot like a purr.

I smiled. I guess I did believe.

Charlotte peeked out from behind the tree again. Maybe making friends was a brave thing that only *looked* easy for some people.

"What should we do?" Gloria asked as Charlotte disappeared behind the tree again.

I thought about how Dad had made being at that birthday party easier for me by giving me the job of acting like a reporter. Maybe it'd be easier for Charlotte if the other Cubs and I gave her a job. "Follow me," I whispered.

Slowly, Gloria, Gordon, and I made our way toward Charlotte, throwing pieces of food to the crows as we went.

"Hey," I called out as we neared the tree. "We have lots of peanuts in here. Can you help us?"

Gloria held out her basket. "C'mon," she said, "we can start thinking about the next issue."

Her face flushing red, Charlotte came out from behind the tree to join us.

That afternoon, we met in the newsroom.

Thom and Min sat by Stuff. Gloria and Gordon arrived together. Charlotte was last to come through the barn doors. "Everyone should file their stories by the end of the day," I said, ignoring the groans. "Remember what I told you about *who, what, where, when,* and *why.*"

Thom and Gloria nodded. "That's true for you, too," I said to Gordon. "We'll need complete info on the photo captions."

We made a plan for everyone to email me their stories first, which I'd edit and then pass on to Charlotte. Then they'd go to Min to lay out.

Min's dad had given us permission to make fifty copies of the paper using his printer, which had better color ink than Mom's. We'd divvy up Bear Creek into routes to distribute the paper on Saturday morning. "Eventually, we'll get some advertisers," I said with a shudder.

"We're really doing this!" Min bounced on the hay bale. Stuff shoved her with his head, making her slip off. I quickly turned my chuckle into a cough. "We're making the newspaper."

Then she danced a little. Or maybe we both did.

CHAPTER FOURTEEN

THE FIRST STORY TO come in was from Gloria.

Bored with the same old, same old? So are *some* people at Wells Diner!!! So we're hosting a recipe competition for diners to try out new dishes!

Send in your favorite dinner or lunch recipe, and we will make it one of our daily specials! Seriously, people, put down the turkey sandwich! Put down the plain cheese pizza! Get over your tomato soup! Give me some jambalaya or curry or something other than what's on the menu at every other diner everywhere in the world!!!

Staff and patrons will vote on the best recipes, which will be a permanent menu item this fall! Save your palate! Save your servers from death by boredom!!! Send us your recipes!

For being such a serious person, Gloria sure did like exclamation points. I deleted all of them, replacing them with periods, and then made a note to her to add more details. *Maybe include some current favorites?*

Soon she wrote back that the current favorites were all boring and flavorless. But she did add: *Chef Wells would like to inform readers that current menu items will continue to be offered despite the plentitude of exciting new recipe options we hope to have available soon.*

Mom read over my shoulder as I edited. She suggested asking Min to create a little box with all of the most important information (when and how to enter) as a graphic. I included a small picture of Gloria, too, to run with the column, since it was an opinion piece.

Gordon sent me a bunch of pictures of Mrs. Austin with the birds and the shot of the bird with the wiper blade rubber to run with my article. I opened a blank page and stared at it, trying to figure out where to start with my park article. Soon I heard, "Starting a story doesn't take a lot of creativity." Mom squeezed my shoulder. "Just answer five questions—*Who? What? When? Where? Why?*" I wondered if she had thought the words in Dad's voice, too.

I turned back to the blank document. *Bear Creek Park is reopened after closing for a few days due to a streak of mischief and possible vandalism that turned out to be*—here Dad would say to hook the reader with something clever—*a murder case. A murder of crows, that is.*

Mom squeezed my shoulder again. "Perfect! But can you one hundred percent for sure say it was just the crows?"

I backspaced and swapped *that seems to have been* for *that turned out to be.*

I was just finishing my article and about to send it and Gloria's column to Charlotte when my inbox pinged with Thom's piece on Miss Juliet.

I had eaten dinner at Thom's house last night (shepherd's pie with brownies for dessert), and he hadn't wanted to talk about the article. He said he had to "think on it" awhile. His moms told me that he had spent the whole day sitting in the dining room with their laptop, clacking away.

I took a deep breath. Who knew what ole Bag of Smells would put in an article? I read it. And I read it again. Then again.

"I'll be back," I said to Mom, who was reading on the couch behind my desk. "I need to talk with Thom."

"Everything okay?" Mom asked.

I didn't answer—just told her I'd be back soon.

The night was clear with the stars so bright it reminded me of an old game, Lite-Brite, at my grandparents' house. It was a light screen that I covered in black construction paper and then poked pegs in so yellow light could shine through while I created my own constellations. I didn't bother calling out Thom's name. I had a feeling where I'd find him.

Gathering up all my courage and swallowing it down inside, I scrambled up a hay bale and then stretched for the low awning of the barn roof where it sloped down in the back.

Letting out a giant breath of panicky air, I lay on my back and slid over to where Thom was watching the stars with Stuff.

If you didn't think about how a fall from eight feet high would certainly result in a broken bone or worse, I supposed it wasn't bad up there. We lay side by side not speaking for a long time, just watching the stars.

"I read your article," I finally said.

Thom's piece focused on when Miss Juliet had been a kid, when she and her mom would make ice cream together. He wrote about how her mom had taught her to make ice cream the same way that her grandmother had made it with *her* mother—generation after generation of women making sweet treats together.

He wrote about all the people who went to the creamery to celebrate or to be with friends. The article only mentioned the happy, not the sad. Just one sentence mentioned that her mom had died five years ago and that now she made the ice cream alone.

Thom kept his chin pointed toward the sky, his shaggy hair falling around the sides of his face.

"You didn't say that she's sad," I said.

"That's because I don't want her to be anymore," Thom said. "She should remember the happy, too."

Next to Thom and Stuff, I watched the Lite-Brite sky without saying anything for a long time. Then, I whispered, "My dad's not in Asia."

"I know," Thom whispered back.

"I miss him."

Thom shuffled a little closer so our arms were resting against each other from shoulder to pinky finger, but neither of us talked. Not even when I cried.

The next morning, I knocked on the door of Bear Creek Creamery ten minutes before it was supposed to open. When Miss Juliet opened the door, pausing to flip the sign hanging inside of it from *Closed* to *Open,* I said, "I'm Nellie Murrow—"

"I know who you are," Miss Juliet said. "We talked last week."

"I'm the editor of *The Cub Report,*" I finished, making sure she knew this was official business. "I want to double-check a few details about the profile we're running on you."

Miss Juliet didn't smile, but she let me into the shop.

"How come all your flavors sound so happy?" I blurted.

"This is for the article?" she replied as she positioned a hairnet over her ponytail.

I nodded, even though it was a lie.

Miss Juliet looked at the framed picture by the register, the one of her with an older woman, both smiling as they held ice cream cones. "I'm trying to taste it."

I looked down at my shoes and tucked my notebook back into my pocket. "Can you?"

I didn't need to look up to know she was shaking her head. "The more I try to cover up how I really feel, the more bitter-sweet stuff tastes. I had a moment the other day, talking with Thom, where I almost had it."

"How long has it been gone? The happy, I mean."

Miss Juliet stared down at the floor for a long moment. I started to think she wasn't going to answer me. "Five years."

My breath sucked into my mouth.

We stood there silently for a moment, then Miss Juliet handed me a hairnet. "Let's try something different today." She flipped the sign hanging in the front door back to *Closed*.

A few hours later, Miss Juliet and I sat down at one of her bistro tables. In front of us was a bowl of Melancholy Mango sorbet and Sour Cherry Sorrow. We didn't speak as we dipped our spoons into the bowls, tasting both flavors.

I gasped at how sweet they tasted, even though while we mixed ingredients, Miss Juliet had talked only about how she still sometimes called her mom's cell phone before going to bed at night.

I told her the truth I had been hiding from everyone, especially myself. Dad had been hit by a car while crossing one of the busy city streets. I told her how it had happened more than a year ago, but that I could still hear his voice. I still felt him with me when I did something we had always done together— like hang out at the park or work at the newspaper.

"I pretend I can talk to my dad when I'm on the swings at the park," I said, then let a little of the ice cream melt on my tongue before finishing. "It works best when I fly so high I feel like I'm going to crash into Heaven."

"That makes sense," Miss Juliet said. "I talk to Mama when I'm in the car driving back from the shop. I pretend she's on the phone and I'm just updating her the way I used to, even on days we had worked side by side."

"My mom talks to Dad all the time," I whispered. "I hear her. Sometimes it hurts, knowing she can talk to him all the time."

We ate more ice cream. Miss Juliet laughed when our spoons knocked with a clang. She was beautiful when she smiled. "Maybe we could talk to each other. Anytime you want."

"I'd like that," I said as I finished the bowl of Sour Cherry Sorrow. It was sweeter than it sounded, but not as sweet as the Hopeful Honey sample she shared with me before I left.

Maybe that Hopeful Honey had filled me up more than I thought, because when Min skipped down the walkway toward me on the way home, I skipped back toward her.

"Charlotte's on her way over," she said. We had planned a design/editing meeting to go over the details of the newspaper to make sure we hadn't made any mistakes.

The headline across the top was *Park mischief key to helping Bear Creek woman.* Gordon's picture of the crows surrounding Mrs. Austin took up a large space. A smaller photo of the crow with the wiper blade in its mouth was beside that image. Along the side of the newspaper was Gloria's now-exclamation-point-free column and graphic. The profile of Miss Juliet was a box under the fold. Next to it was a how-to on making a bag of smells, including another graphic by Min (*Step one: Get a bag. Step two: Find smelly stuff. Step three: Put smelly stuff in bag. Step four: Keep in pocket.*), but I tried not to think about that article too much. On the other side was a small column, this one by me, all about *The Cub Report* and how readers could contact us for future stories.

Min, Charlotte, and I sat at the Kim-Franklins' dining room table, our heads sometimes bumping as we stared at the design on Min's giant computer screen.

After about an hour of combing over the newspaper, with Charlotte quietly pointing out lots of missing commas and all three of us double- and triple-checking spellings, we leaned back in our seats.

"It's a real newspaper," Charlotte said. Min texted Thom, Gloria, and Gordon to see if they wanted to be present for the first printing. Soon, all three were in the kitchen with us.

Min squealed and clapped, then pressed the "publish" button so the paper would appear on the website she and Gordon had created the day before. Then she hit print to make the physical copies we'd distribute in the morning.

As soon as the printer started to churn, I screeched, "Stop the presses!" Both Min and Charlotte yelped so loudly that I laughed until my stomach ached. "Sorry! I have always wanted to say that."

I took the first copy of *The Cub Report* from the printer. Gordon snapped a picture of me holding it in my hands. He showed me the image and then passed the camera to the others to see, too.

"You look different," Min said as she peered at the image.

"I know," I said, and my voice was Hopeful Honey. "I look like my dad."

CHAPTER FIFTEEN

"EXTRA! EXTRA!" MIN SHOUTED as we scootered through Bear Creek. She stopped at each house to stick a rolled-up paper in the mailbox. "*The Cub Report* is a real newspaper! Read all about it!"

"Min!" I shouted from across the street, where I was also distributing the paper. "You don't have to say that it's a real paper. People will think that it's *not* real if you're constantly saying it's real."

"Extra! Extra!" Min shouted louder.

We both paused outside of the ice cream shop. Last night, after I showed her the first copy of *The Cub Report,* Mom had taken me to the creamery to celebrate. Miss Juliet was so excited about her profile that she taped the whole paper in the shop's window. At some point that morning, Miss Juliet had moved the photo beside the register to hang in the window next to the newspaper. Min and I waved at Miss Juliet through the window before continuing toward Wells Diner.

The whole staff had planned out our routes so we could meet at Wells for lunch. Chef Wells had a stack of *The Cub Report* on the counter; the servers slipped one onto each person's tray.

In the corner of the diner was Mrs. Austin, eating soup and bread. Nearly everyone stopped by her table to say how glad they were to see her back at the park. The hardware store owner said he'd make sure there was always a bag of birdseed for her behind the register. She winked at me as I walked by.

My cell phone vibrated in my pocket while I waited in line for a turkey sandwich. I almost ignored it but then heard a ping at the same time coming from Gordon's phone as he stood in front of me in line. I remembered the email we had set up for *The Cub Report* and how each staff member had access to it.

Quickly, I pulled my phone out of my pocket. The message was from Mr. Tran, the ornithologist. *Hey kid!* it began. How rude. But I let that go as I continued reading. *Great job with your article. Saw it online. Glad to hear the murder was trying to tell you something.*

"Nellie!" came a gruff voice behind me, followed by a slurp. Chief Rodgers. I turned to see him sitting with a copy of *The Cub Report* in one hand. His soup spoon was in the other. "You done good, kid."

"Thank you," I said in my grout voice. "Just doing my job."

"Almost sorry to hear this is all wrapped up. I was getting used to seeing you around," Chief Rodgers said.

"Oh, we'll still be around. We're publishing monthly," I said before remembering to use my official voice. Much lower, I added, "I have an associate"—that would be Mom—"who has provided us with a police scanner. *The Cub Report* will be ready and on the scene for any Bear Creek breaking news."

Gordon turned toward me as Chief Rodgers grumbled into his napkin.

"What *are* we going to cover in the next issue?" Gordon asked.

Thom pushed his bag of smells into his back pocket. I noticed it now had a corner from *The Cub Report* tucked inside. "Well, Mom says Annabelle keeps going on rampages, destroying gardens in town."

"Annabelle?" I asked, already taking notes.

"The potbelly pig," Gordon finished.

I stopped taking notes. "Well, hopefully something more exciting than an escaped pig will happen in the next couple weeks."

Just then Chief Rodgers's walkie-talkie buzzed. "All units, all units! Possible burglary on Olson Avenue. Who can report?"

"*Me!*" I yelled as Chief Rodgers responded that he was on his way.

"Not now, Nellie," Chief Rodgers growled as he threw money on the table and gathered up his things.

"You can't stop the press!" I told him. He sighed and didn't even offer me a lift. That's okay. I can make my scooter go nearly as fast as I can swing.

But by the time I got out to the curb, Gordon was sailing down the sidewalk on his skateboard, following the police cars. Already his camera was snapping pictures.

The Cub Report was ready for its next assignment.

AP/Associated Press: a nonprofit news agency headquartered in New York City. American newspapers and broadcasters are members. The AP shares news articles among its members and sets the standard for newspaper style, or how newspapers consistently phrase and order items in articles.

beat: a topic or area that a reporter covers. Beats include municipal (town news), crime or police, lifestyle or features, or niche topics, such as music or food.

the big five: the five questions all journalists must answer in news articles: *who, what, where, when,* and *why*

columnist: a person who works at a newspaper and writes an opinion piece

copy: unedited articles or columns

copy editor: someone who reads over copy—articles—and points out mistakes

cub reporter: a new journalist

editorial board: the members of a newspaper in charge of writing opinion pieces on behalf of the newspaper

First Amendment: this amendment to the US Constitution promises freedom of the press to follow stories.

freelancer: a reporter who is not employed by a specific newspaper but who is hired to write specific articles

lede: the first paragraph of a news story. In most cases, a journalist would aim to answer who, what, where, when, and why in the lede.

masthead: the design and name of the newspaper at the top of each issue

Nellie Bly: the pen name of Elizabeth Cochran Seaman, a journalist who lived from 1864 to 1922. Bly is often credited with founding investigative journalism and is famous for posing as a patient to expose unethical practices in a mental asylum.

objectivity: the concept of not taking a slant or side to a story but presenting the facts fairly for the reader

on the record: information or interviews that can be used in an article (off the record: information or interviews that cannot be used in an article. Sometimes sources will provide off-the-record interviews if providing an interview will pose risk to them personally or professionally. This lets journalists know to scout out different sources who might be on the record.)

scoop: to be the first journalist or newspaper to share information

sources: people or institutions that provide information for articles

top of the fold: the stories above a folded-in-half newspaper. Generally, these are the most important stories in the issue.

ACKNOWLEDGMENTS

Growing up, I'd sit beside my dad as he read the *York Daily Record/Sunday News* cover to cover every night. Years later, I'd have a byline in that same newspaper. Some nights Mom or Dad would call and say, "You won't believe what I read in the paper!" and then read from an article I had written. I loved being a journalist, how every day was different, every story new, and how everything could change with one ping of the police scanner.

The newsroom taught me to question everything; that ethics never bend; that every person has a story; and, most importantly of all, that every story matters. Those years as a reporter were among the best and hardest of my life.

My editor, Julie Matysik, and Val Howlett, children's senior publicity and marketing manager, first dreamed up *The Newspaper Club* idea. When they shared it with me, I bounced more than that baby Min! I'm so lucky to be working with both of them, along with the rest of the RPK team, including cover and interior designer Marissa Raybuck, project manager Amber Morris, copy editor Christina Palaia, associate publisher Jessica Schmidt, and publisher Kristin Kiser. Thank you Paula Franco for the incredible illustrations of the Cubs.

Thank you to super agent and super human Nicole Resciniti for being such a powerful advocate, resource, and friend.

And, of course, tremendous love to my family and friends for making this dream job possible.

A Sneak Peek at

Beth Vrabel's Next Book in

the Newspaper Club Series:

The Cubs Get
the Scoop

CHAPTER ONE

I CLAPPED MY HANDS to get the attention of the news staff. They were too busy chatting with each other or feeding Stuff (the goat) to pay attention to their editor (me).

"All right, guys. We have three weeks until school starts. Just enough time to release another issue. What's on the budget?"

"Budget?" Thom was sitting on a hay bale next to Stuff. Technically speaking, the newsroom was Thom's barn.

"Newspaper budgets don't have anything to do with money," I explain. "It's a breakdown of the stories that we're planning—or budgeting for—in the next issue."

"But what about the other kind of budget? Are walkie talkies in that budget?" Min asked as she pulled the ruffles of her dress out of Stuff's mouth. Min lived next to me and across the street from Thom, wore ruffles on every outfit, and was prone to dotting the *i* in her name with a heart.

"I do *not* have money for this," Gloria said. She crossed her thin arms and narrowed her eyes. Gloria was wearing the blue jersey-style uniform shirt from her shift at the Wells Diner, the restaurant downtown that her dad owned. "No one said we needed money to be on the newspaper."

"None of us have money," I pointed out. We lived in Bear Creek, Maine. Think of a super hip urban area in a city and then make everything the total opposite. That's Bear Creek. No one is rich, but Min's family came close. Her whole family went to Disney World every summer—grandparents, aunts and uncles, cousins. This year, her aunties from Korea joined them, too. (Even her dad had been wearing mouse ears when they had gotten back from the airport last week. My dad would never do that. *It's called dignity,* I heard his voice in my mind. But I knew that I was just expressing my thoughts in his voice. The truth is, Dad totally would've worn mouse ears. But he would've also pointed out that commercial vacations were an indulgence that shouldn't be repeated.)

I cleared my throat. "We don't have a budget about money, just articles we're planning. Besides, we don't need walkie talkies, Min. We all have cell phones."

"Walkie talkies are more fun." Min crossed her arms.

"Oh," Gloria said. "I'm okay with story budgets." Her long brown hair was braided in cornrows except for her bangs, which she blew off her forehead with a puff. The purple and silver beads at the ends of her braids clicked when she shrugged.

Gordon pushed off the hay bale next to Gloria and leaned against the side of the barn, looking out over Thom's yard. His mom, Dr. Burke, was the superintendent of Bear Creek School District. Dr. Burke and Gordon were a lot alike; and not just because of their looks (both had wide smiles, brown skin, and freckles). They also had something about them that made people around them sit up and take notice. Dad would call them charismatic. I bet Gordon's family didn't worry about going on vacation, either. They had a red brick house in Foxcroft Estates, the part of town where people hired landscapers to mow their lawn into long stripes. Mrs. Kim-Franklin told Mom they'd live there but the homes "lacked character." (I think she just wanted to let people know that they could afford fancy grass.)

"I have money," Min said, as though she had read my thoughts. At ten, Min is younger than the rest of us, which might explain her affinity for ruffles and pastel colors. I am almost twelve. I wear black and gray as a matter of principle.

Right then Min was wearing a lavender sundress with a ruffle across the chest. She also wore white sneakers with, you guessed it, white ruffled socks. Even her purple headband was ruffled where it lay against her dark hair. Min opened the small mouse-eared backpack resting by her feet and pulled out a twenty-dollar bill. Waving it in the air, she said, "I got allowance last night. Why don't we go to the creamery?"

"You got back from vacation yesterday," I said. "How could you have possibly earned an allowance?"

Min shrugged. "I get paid every Monday."

"For what?"

"For being a kid."

I once pulled every weed in the flower gardens surrounding our old farmhouse—even got scraped on the huge yellow rosebush by the front door—and all I got was a ten-dollar bill from Mom.

"Do you want ice cream or not?" Min asked.

"Of course, I want ice cream," I snapped. Everyone jumped to their feet, even Charlotte, who had been sitting in a shadowy corner of the barn reading the *AP Stylebook* like the dream copy editor she was.

"Wait!" I snapped. "We don't have time for ice cream right now. We have to figure out the next issue."

"Well, we have the Annabelle story," Thom pointed out. He must've noticed Gloria blowing on her forehead because he turned on an old metal fan in the corner of the barn. Stuff rammed forward and stood directly in front of the breeze, emitting goat-scented air throughout the barn. Charlotte leaned over and unplugged the fan, making everyone laugh. Soon Charlotte's face was as red as her hair. She was super quiet. Even after weeks of hanging out in the barn—I mean, newsroom—I still didn't know her well.

I sighed. Annabelle lived a couple blocks from the newsroom in a little Cape Cod house where everything looked even neater and cleaner than Min's house—and Mrs. Kim-Franklin vacuums every afternoon at three o'clock. Of course, Annabelle tended to be pretty dirty and covered in food. That's because she's a pig.

Annabelle had a habit of rummaging through neighbors' gardens. In fact, on the day that *The Cub Report* became a real newspaper, with issues being given to everyone in Bear Creek, all police were called to the scene of a break-in . . . which ended up being Annabelle pushing through the front door of a neighbor's house to get to a freshly baked pie.

"No one's going to take *The Cub Report* seriously if our top-of-the-fold story is a pig pie theft."

"But we don't fold our newspaper. We roll it." Min still was waving her twenty-dollar bill.

I sighed again.

"The Wrinkler family was at the diner last night," Gloria said. "They told me Annabelle helped herself to their garden carrots last night. And then the Thompsons said she ate all their lettuce. But the Thompsons aren't all that reliable. When they went to pay the tab, Mr. Thompsons couldn't find his wallet and Mrs. Thompsons forgot her purse, so Dad had to put their meal on a tab. Again."

"All right," I said. "We've got to follow the news, even if it's boring. Thom, how about you cover the Annabelle story? Remember, keep it to the big six."

Every news story had to cover *who, what, where, when, how,* and *why*.

Thom nodded and walked toward the barn doors.

"Where are you going?" I asked.

"To interview Annabelle," he said.

"You can't interview Annabelle."

"Why not?" Thom asked.

"Well, for starters, because she's a pig. Besides, you don't even have a notebook!" I always have a reporter's notebook and two pens in my back pocket. Thom's cut-off jean shorts had a huge hole in the back pocket. I handed him a notebook from my backpack, and a blue and red pen. He tucked a pen behind each ear, pulling back the sides of his shaggy blond hair, and headed out.

Thom's different than anyone I had ever met. I was pretty sure he would've interviewed a pig. He was a careful writer and he noticed things a lot of people overlooked. I'd make a journalist out of him yet.

Gordon pushed off the side of the barn. He kicked on the edge of his skateboard, popping it up so he could grab it with his outstretched hand. With the other, he shifted the camera hanging on his neck. "I'll catch up to Thom—maybe get a shot of Annabelle in action."

I looked down at the budget list. So far, it only had Annabelle on it.

My heart hammered as I thought about *The Bear Creek Gazette*, the town newspaper that had closed for good earlier this month. Now *The Cub Report* was the only independent press in town; if we couldn't make this newspaper work, no one would have access to local news.

"Did you hear what happened in Burlington Meadows?" Gloria asked.

Burlington Meadows was a town about two hours south of us. Mom and I had spent the night there when we moved from the city. I remember thinking it was a teeny tiny town only to discover it's twice the size of Bear Creek. But surely even exciting things happen in teeny tiny towns, right? Things other than pie-stealing pigs?

"What happened?" Min asked, bouncing on her toes. She had a tendency to bounce. Sometimes she even skipped. Despite this, she was a good friend, even if she did argue with me way more than necessary.

"Well, you know how there's a prison in Windham?"

"Yes!" Min and I said at the same time, though I was pretty sure neither of us had known that.

Gloria leaned forward, her elbow on her knee. Her eyebrows peaked and her mouth twitched. Gloria always knew everything going on in town thanks to the diner, and she loved dishing it out. Her writing would benefit from fewer exclamation points, though; I could hear them when she talked, too. "Well, some prisoners were being transferred to another location, right? And the van stopped in Burlington Meadows for gas. Somehow a prisoner *escaped*! He's been loose ever since! There are, like, a million police officers in Burlington Meadows. They even have hound dogs searching for the guy's scent!"

"Wow," Charlotte whispered.

The four of us looked at each other, all thinking the same thing: *Why couldn't anything like that happen here in Bear Creek?*

An escaped prisoner? That was a top-of-the-fold news story for sure.

There's never a shortage of news, just a lack of insight. This was one of my dad's favorite sayings. He'd tell it to any reporter who complained about not having a story. *Go out and find one. Everyone has a story.*

"Everyone has a story," I said aloud. "There are lots of interesting stories right here in Bear Creek, I'm sure. We just have to leave the newsroom, meet people, and scout out their stories."

"I'm not allowed to talk to strangers," Min said. She waved her money again. "I *am* allowed to get ice cream."

Gloria tilted her head toward Min and nodded. "Same."

"Min, it's not talking with strangers if you're a reporter. It's literally the job," I said.

"It's literally going to get me in trouble," Min said and crossed her arms. She looked a lot like her mom when she did that.

Gloria fanned herself with the back of her hand and blew air up on her bangs again. "As someone who works with the Bear Creek public on the regular, I can tell you that some people's stories are that they're boring and need to get a life. Kind of like we need to get ice cream."

I stood and put my hands on my hips. "I could go anywhere in Bear Creek, meet anyone, and have a story by tonight. It's all in the questions."

"Prove it," Charlotte suddenly said. She strolled over to the map of Bear Creek on the barn wall and studied it for a second. "If everyone has a story, like you say, go here"—she pointed to an intersection on the far western corner of Bear Creek—"and find the person who lives there. Get their story."

Quiet Charlotte suddenly looked fierce. "Prove it."

CHAPTER TWO

WHEN I LIVED IN the city, I had my own subway pass. And I was only ten.

Now I'm nearly twelve and live in a town whose whole population is less than my previous school district, but when Charlotte pointed to a random intersection on the north side of town, I wasn't exactly sure it'd be okay for me to go there by myself.

In the city, I never felt alone because there were moms and dads pushing strollers, shops with open signs in the windows, and police officers on nearly every block. Bear Creek had actual *bears*. It also had long, long stretches of lonely woods without cell phone reception.

I reminded myself that I was named after Nellie Bly, the founder of investigative journalism. *That* Nellie traveled the whole world by herself; she wouldn't be nervous about going a couple miles outside of town. Not that I was scared. However, today did seem like a nice day for a walk with a friend. "So, who's coming with me?" I asked the Cubs.

"Sorry." Min tucked her allowance into her pocket. "I have plans."

"Me too," Gloria said.

Charlotte, her cheeks still pink from speaking so loudly, lowered her head.

"Do your plans happen to be getting ice cream?" I asked.

Min smiled.

I straightened my back. "Okay. I'll do the *lead* feature this issue. And you guys maybe won't even have an article. That's *fine*."

Gloria turned to Min. "I heard Miss Juliet added a new flavor—Bittersweet Mint—to the creamery. I think that's what I'm going to get."

I growled. Neither Min nor Gloria looked my way. Charlotte continued to study her dirty canvas sneakers. "Charlotte?"

She shook her head. "I think I have some copy editing to do."

"We don't have any stories yet. How could you edit stories that haven't been written?"

Charlotte's birdlike shoulders peaked and fell.

"Fine." I paused to study the map.

"Corner of Appleyard and Morgan Roads," Charlotte whispered.

"I know." I snapped a picture of the map with my cell phone. I marched toward the barn doors, but slowly, in case any of them felt the immense guilt that should've accompanied calling out their editor and then leaving her to write a story on her own. The three continued discussing Bittersweet Mint.

Know what I love? Mint ice cream.

Everyone has a story, I heard in Dad's voice. With a heavy sigh that no one seemed to notice, I trudged across the street to my house so I could tell Mom I was heading out for a story.

This is what my life had come to: skipping ice cream *and* checking in with my mom. The price for quality journalism in a small town is high.

Mom wasn't home.

Fact: Mom was *always* home.

Since we moved from the city, she spent all day in the attic. Not because she had turned into a bat or anything; she was working on a book, or at least that was what she told me. I was pretty sure she was working on not missing Dad so much.

My dad had been an incredible journalist. I know how to be the *Cub Report* news editor because he had been the news editor of a major newspaper. People listened to Dad. Not because he was loud—he almost never raised his voice (except when someone forgot to fill the coffeepot). People cared about what he had to say because he was smart and he was careful, especially with other people's stories. That made him important.

I wanted to be like that. I *was* going to be like that, starting with this story, the one I was going to scout out in the middle of nowhere, Bear Creek.

I texted Mom. *Hey, where are you?*

The three dots danced on my screen instantly. *I'm at the creamery getting coffee with Juliet. All ok?*

For a moment, everything turned black. What kind of bittersweet mint misery was this? Everyone getting ice cream but me? I growled so loudly the sound echoed in the empty attic.

Something scurried in a corner. I tried not to think about what it could be.

Fine. I texted back. I took a deep breath. *Tell Miss Juliet I say hi.* It was a good thing Mom and Miss Juliet were hanging out. *The Cub Report* kind of brought them together, I guess. Our first issue had profiled the ice-cream maker. Thom's reporting shared that Miss Juliet's mother had died a few years earlier. So, she and Mom had something in common; both were mourning. Something squished in my heart. I missed Dad so much that I didn't have words for it. (And as the daughter of two journalists, I always had words.)

Sometimes I let myself believe Dad was simply on a long business trip to Asia. I had stopped telling other people that—it seemed to make them really worried. But it's the story I told myself sometimes.

I straightened my back and sent another text to Mom. *Going to interview someone for the paper. Corner of Morgan and Appleyard Roads. Okay?* Mom must've been enjoying her ice cream because I didn't see the three dots. I tucked the phone into my backpack, then trotted down the steps to the kitchen for a bottle of water. On a hot day like this, cool water was even better than ice cream.

That's a lie.

I tucked the water bottle into my bag, made sure I had my notebook and two pens, then hopped on my bike and headed toward Morgan Road.

Dad would be excited to hear about how I scouted out a story all by myself.

———————————————

Appleyard Road was farther away than I had thought. A few times, I tried to pull up the map on my phone just to make sure I was heading in the right direction.

As I pedaled up Morgan Road, the street became narrower. Pine trees soared toward a clear blue sky on both sides. The grass bordering the road was patchy and tall. Birds chirped all around and squirrels darted in front of me like they had never seen a bicycle before. A few cars and pickup trucks passed, but the farther I pedaled, the fewer signs of human life I saw. The way was almost uphill the entire time. I tried not to think about how I was going to have to go down the hill to get home. Fact: I'd always pick going uphill over downhill.

Gravity was so bossy.

Some people (ahem, Min) say that *I'm* bossy. That's not true. I'm reliably right and thoughtful in my approach.

Finally, I saw the Appleyard Road sign. I stepped off the bike and stood at the intersection, looking around. If I was going to tell someone's story from this part of town, I was going to have to find a person, and *that* was going to be tricky, given there was only one house in sight. And that house looked, well, kind of scary.

I sucked on my bottom lip, considering.

I got out my notebook, flipped to a fresh page, and wrote. *Lots of weeds along very long driveway.* Then I scratched out the word *very*. Once I overheard Dad tell a reporter that *very* was a tool for lazy writers. It actually made something weaker to write it. The reporter had written that it was very difficult for someone to get a permit in the city. *If it's difficult, say it's difficult. Saying it's* very *difficult introduces the idea that some things might be* more *difficult,* Dad had told her.

The driveway was long, stretching back and curving slightly so I could just barely make out the house at the end. Again, I turned to my notebook. *Grand-looking house. White, or at least, once was white. Now grayish. Two stories with black shutters and a huge wraparound porch.* I squinted down the driveway. *One rocker on the porch.* Though the house was much larger than the little old farmhouse Mom and I lived in, something about it reminded me of home. If I tilted my head when looking at my house, I could see glimmers of how it had looked when new. This house, I bet, once had been glorious.

"Well, are you going to go or not?"

I immediately looked up. People in Bear Creek had a habit of hanging out in trees. I unsnapped my helmet to make sure I could see. But no one was in the trees around me. Instead, behind me stood a small, older woman. Quickly, I scribbled in my notebook: *Woman with long white hair. Walking stick. Angry voice.*

"Are you writing about me, young lady?" the woman asked.

"No," I blurted. "I mean, yes." I slipped the pen into the ring of the notebook and thrust out my hand to shake hers. Her hand was strong and callused, and it surprised me. I guess I was expecting soft, tissue-thin skin like my grandma's. "I'm Nellie Murrow, news editor of *The Cub Report*."

The woman's eyebrows mushed together and so did her lips. "*The Cub Report?*"

"It's a real newspaper."

"Is that right?" the woman replied. "I'm Patricia Wilkonson. A reporter, huh? Well, then, I assume you're here to talk to me about my pen. I wondered if I'd hear from the media today."